Office in Back

**Falling in love is the easy part.
Negotiating the living is the hard part.**

Linda L. Harley

Grateful Steps
Asheville, North Carolina

Grateful Steps Foundation
Crest Mountain
30 Ben Lippen School Road #107
Asheville, North Carolina 28806

Library of Congress Control Number 2018904753
Harley, Linda L.
Office in Back:
Falling in love is the easy part.
Negotiating the living is the hard part.

Cover design by David Sheldon
Sheldon Studioworks, Asheville, North Carolina
https://www.facebook.com/TheArtOfDavidSheldon/

ISBN 978-1-945714-18-4 Paperback

Printed in the United States of America
at Lightning Source

FIRST EDITION

Publisher's Cataloging-In-Publication Data
Prepared by The Donohue Group, Inc.
Names: Harley, Linda L.
Title: Office in back : falling in love is the easy part. Negotiating the living is the hard part / Linda L. Harley.
Description: First edition. | Asheville, North Carolina : Grateful Steps, [2018]
Identifiers: ISBN 9781945714184 (paperback) | ISBN 9781945714290 (ebook)
Subjects: LCSH: Marital conflict--Fiction. | Married people--Psychology--Fiction. | Marriage counseling--Fiction. | LCGFT: Domestic fiction.
Classification: LCC PS3608.A74428 O34 2018 (print) | LCC PS3608.A74428 (ebook) | DDC 813/.6--dc23

www.gratefulsteps.org

In Memory:

Dedicated to Dr. J. Crit Harley: my husband, I will always love forever and a day.

Without his unfaltering support in countless ways, this book would have never been written.

Acknowledgments:

Tevya Harley, my daughter: who is always a telephone call away.

Elizabeth F. Little (Betty), teacher and mentor: who gave me the foundation to be the counselor I have become.

The late Stephen Black, *Hendersonville Times-News* columnist of "On Borrowed Time": who read my manuscript in its rawest form and gave me ideas to enrich my work.

Ann B. Ross, author and friend: who encouraged me to keep on "revising" and stated, "You finally have a story."

David Sheldon (Sheldon Studioworks), artist and illustrator: who made the time to do the cover art for *Office in Back.*

Grateful Steps Publishing House: believed in my novel, *Office in Back*, and took time to invest in a new author. Rebecca Muller and Patrick Graff, Grateful Steps interns: who helped process corrections received from the much appreciated copy editor, Cathy Mitchell. Ph.D.

Peter Yarrow, singer and songwriter: who gave permission to include in my novel the second verse of the song, "Light One Candle."

Preface:

Office in Back is a novel I had to write. Because of my work as a couple's counselor, I have been given the gift by my clients to appreciate the normalcy of every couple's struggles and concerns:

- that no one marries to get a divorce.
- that every couple's dream is to grow very old together, go happily into the sunset, "till death do us part."

Linda L. Hanley

Contents:

Prologue

The Fight

"Damn it, what do you want from me?" I stated emphatically. I hit the top of the dresser with my fist. "One day you say you love me, and you couldn't be happier. Next day you're yelling at me, telling me I don't do shit, and you were happier single. I can't win!"

"I do love you, but what does it take to get your attention and your time?" She screeched, her face red with anger, "You're the most aggravating person on the face of the earth. Do I have to tell you everything? You should know something about me by now! Do you just not care, or are you just stupid?"

"Now, I'm stupid, huh?" My voice lowered to a hardened chill, as my question forced itself through my clenched teeth. "Well, let me tell you a thing or two. You're never satisfied. If I ask you a question to clarify things, you get pissed. If I guess wrong as to what you're cooking up in that weird brain of yours, I'm pounded for not asking. Damned if I do and damned if I don't! Why try?"

"I'm weird now. You're the weird one! My friends tell me they wouldn't put up with your crap!" She raged, an octave higher than her screech.

"So go live with *them*." I stated harshly.

"This is hell fighting like this with you! I won't do this anymore! What's happened to us? You're not the man I married. We hardly speak anymore, much less do anything together." She stopped abruptly. Tears quickly erupted from her eyes and poured over her cheeks, splashing down onto the front of her bathrobe.

I slammed the bathroom door and turned on the shower. Maybe a cold shower would cool off my rage, and if I took a long shower, maybe she'd be asleep by the time I was done.

Chapter One
The Morning Jog

DESPITE THE BRISK EARLY MORNING, SWEAT DRIPPED DOWN my face as I jogged familiar streets. I pushed myself harder than normal, trying to outrun the thoughts that dogged my every step. My rhythm was off, and I stopped underneath a large, bright red oak tree and leaned against it, the autumn sun warm on my face. I stared vacantly at the Carolina blue sky, and the patchwork quilts of bright gold, orange, red and yellow fall trees that blanketed the Blue Ridge Mountains, which circled the small town I now call home. I fought back the emotions swelling to choke me. Ironic, me, hard ass C.J. Alfred was always in rhythm, always in control.

Last night, Leeta and I had another one of those loud and mean arguments that lasted for hours. I can't even remember what started it all, but I remember the hurtful things said in the heat of anger. The things couples say that later they didn't mean, yet they ring with a bit of truth, despite the protests that say differently. Like alcohol, anger has a way of loosening the tongue.

Leeta and I have been married for five years. This is the second marriage for us both. She was thirty-five with a ten-year-old son when we were married. I was forty-two. We both vowed on our wedding day, "till death do us part" and meant it. However, at the rate we are going our death and parting might not be due to the grace of old age but due to our own rage.

A car honked, jolting me out of my bittersweet memories. I looked down at my watch. It was eight-thirty in the morning, thirty minutes since I leaned myself against this oak tree. Except now, I found myself sitting at its broad base. The sweat that had dripped from my forehead earlier had now dried, sticky on my stubble. What must I look like unshaven and weary to the people driving by, taking kids to school and going to work? It would be no surprise either, if Leeta saw me as she took Travis, my stepson, to his school.

I stood up slowly, noting how stiff my entire body felt. I took in deep slow breaths to regain my legendary control. I needed to make sense of what was happening again and why. I had loved two women in my adult life and married both. Cullen, my first wife, I hadn't thought of in years until I inadvertently saw one of her children's books in the local bookstore on Main Street. I had felt pride in her accomplishments and a loving feeling that both surprised and alarmed me. I had not thought of Cullen again until last night's argument. "You're not the man I married," Leeta said with tears running down her face. "What's happened to us? We hardly speak anymore, much less do anything together."

Cullen had said almost those exact words twelve years prior with her suitcases in hand just before she walked out of my life. The fighting had grown intense between Cullen and me. The lovemaking had stopped. I thought her selfish and irrational. In my early thirties and having no children, I chalked it up as a mistake. I simply let her walk away without any thought to reconcile. Now, for the first time, I am asking myself what exactly went wrong between us. At the time we married, I would have told you it was the best decision of my life. If you had asked me when I married Leeta, I would have said the same thing.

I bent my body back, arms akimbo with hands placed on my hips, stretching this way and that to flex and loosen my stiff muscles. I repeated these movements a few more times, before I felt I was ready to put my body in forward motion. I walked down the street past the doctors' offices and found myself staring at a sign. It read:

JANE H. LEVY, MSW, LCSW, PLLC
LICENSED MARRIAGE AND FAMILY THERAPIST.
OFFICE IN BACK.

Chapter Two

Office in Back

I'VE JOGGED THIS STREET ALMOST DAILY AND NEVER NOTICED IT. I walked around back and stood staring at the red sign with bold, white letters on the door: Jane H. Levy, MSW, LCSW. Licensed Marriage and Family Therapist.

I saw my right hand turn the doorknob and open the door. I walked in and stood in the middle of a small, unpretentious, but inviting waiting room, almost a cottage effect with white paneled walls. Sunshine streamed in from the windows behind me. Two comfortable chairs had been placed on each side of the room and an old Queen Anne desk sat to the left of me. A table covered with books and articles was between two of the chairs, and a wicker basket filled with magazines was visible between the other two chairs.

I sat down beside the table. I picked up the book, *Serendipity*, and found myself thumbing through its pages, when my eye caught the title of another book, *Kitchen Table Wisdom*. I picked up that book and under it were *Chicken Soup for the Soul* and *14,000 Things to be Happy About*. Beside these books was a copy of a *Newsweek* article with big bold letters reading, **EXHAUSTED**. I lifted up this article and saw the words, "The Power of Prayer," running across the cover of *TIME*

Magazine. Ms. Levy's choices of reading materials were interesting. I heard soft, indistinguishable sounds of voices in the next room, and laughter. What could be funny or fun about being in a marital therapist's office? The laughter became louder as the door opened and three people walked out. An attractive couple, a middle aged man and woman, headed for the door.

"We'll see you in two weeks," they said in unison.

Ms. Levy stood quietly in front of me. Not exactly who I expected. Looking at her, I could not decide whether she was old or young. She was small in stature—petite, in fact—with unusual, muted moss green eyes. Highlighting these eyes was a mop of light brown curls. She smiled and her eyes crinkled. "May I help you?"

"I don't know," I stammered. "I just walked in. Impulse, I guess."

She sat down in the chair across from me and looked directly into my eyes. She furrowed her brows and carefully paraphrased my words. "You don't know if I can help you. You just walked in on an impulse."

"Yes," I stated reluctantly. "I saw your sign on Sixth. I have never noticed it before. Have you been here long?"

"Since May 2000," she replied quietly.

I muttered to myself in dismay, "How many years have I jogged on this street, five years?"

"Excuse me. I didn't hear what you said."

"I should go," I said uncomfortably, but I did not budge from the chair. I heard myself say, "I haven't been happy in my marriage for a long time. Too many fights that last into the wee hours of the morning, and I frequently can't even remember what started the fight in the first place."

"Well, it seems you've come to the right place. Would you like to make an appointment for you and your wife?"

"I haven't talked to her," I reluctantly disclosed. *Now, what do I do or say next?* Just as I was trying to control my swirling thoughts to figure out something to say, the office door opened and an older man walked in with a smile. *Thank you, mister, for your perfect timing.*

"Hello," she said. "I'll be with you in just a moment. Please make yourself comfortable in the other room."

He nodded as he went into the room that the other couple and she had just left. She walked over to the Queen Ann desk and retrieved from holders on top of the desk a pamphlet and a card. She turned toward me. "You and your wife look this over. I'll be happy to work with you two, but now I must excuse myself."

"Thank you," I said as I strained to stand up. I felt I was being held back, as if I was sitting in a pile of sticky crazy glue. The grief I'd felt all morning had taken hold of me, and it frightened me. I never felt so completely emptied out, like someone or something reached inside my chest and tore my heart right out of me. I took the pamphlet from her. She nodded her head and smiled as she turned to walk into the other room. I walked perfunctorily out into the morning sunshine. The brightness of the sunshine, in contrast to my intense internal desolation, was disturbingly weird. My jog quickened, stressing every muscle in my body. I needed desperately to fill the hole in my heart. Turning right onto the dirt drive that led to our house, I grabbed my sweaty shirt and held it tight. My heart was racing hard and fast. I gasped for air and felt the wrenching pain of each breath in, but my God, at least I felt normal.

There stood our two-story, white frame Victorian home with a wraparound porch, complete with horse stable and thirty-five acres of pastureland and woods. In Hendersonville, one never knew what one would find by turning down this road or the next. The surprises were endless, and our horse farm within the town limits was just one of them. One could drive by a lovely development of homes or an aging mansion. Down another road, one could see acres of apple orchards with the Blue Ridge

Mountains as the orchards' backdrop. Or down another road one might see mallards and Canadian geese resting placidly on a pond's surface.

My cell phone rang, reclaiming me from my thoughts, and my hello was answered by a cheerful Kate, "Hi, plan to be in today?"

"Well . . . yeah," I said hesitantly, looking down at my watch. "Jeez, it's almost nine o'clock."

"Yep, sure is. Are you okay?"

"Yes, yes, Kate," I said impatiently.

Kate quickly picked up on my mood. The light, upbeat voice vanished and now was replaced with a voice that echoed caution and concern. "Okay then, you do remember the meeting at one o'clock with the New York architect, George Schwartz, and his assistant?"

"Yes, Kate. I remember. I'll be there within the hour. Bye." Today was a red-letter day for the plant. A big New York City bank was contracting with us to buy our insulation to upgrade their entire heating and plumbing system.

"Good-bye." The phone clicked off. Kate knew me well, over twenty years now. She was my first, and to this day, my most loyal and hardworking employee. She had proclaimed on her sixty-fifth birthday that she had no plans for retirement. "Why, Mother died when she was ninety-six years old. She was able to live on her own until the last six weeks of her life, and then she went downhill fast. I credit her long life to her not sitting down and always having something to sink her teeth into. My plan too, and this company has plenty to keep me busy and interested."

I hurried to shave and shower and placed Ms. Levy's pamphlet and card on my dresser in the bedroom. As I dried myself off, I could hear Leeta downstairs in the kitchen. Hannah, our golden retriever, bounded up the stairs. Since Hannah hadn't greeted me, I had assumed she was in her usual place in the truck with Leeta taking

Travis to school. Hannah was always ready for a ride in anybody's vehicle. There was no loyalty there.

Hannah was four now, and her energy was boundless, a definite trademark of the golden. She knew all the standard commands of come, sit, stay, down and heel— Leeta's requirement for a housedog. I didn't object. Travis and I taught Hannah to retrieve the ball. A big mistake, because once the game was started, Hannah didn't want to quit. Travis and I also taught her to retrieve the newspaper. This was not a mistake for she was satisfied to retrieve the paper only once, unlike her ball. In what I still believe was a moment of genius, I added training Hannah to retrieve my reading glasses. I was forever misplacing them and wasting time looking for them. Though usually wet from slobber, they have to date, been delivered intact. As I was putting on my shoes and asking Hannah to fetch my glasses, Leeta extended her hand with my glasses in tow. "Thanks," I said, taking the glasses from her.

"They were still on your dresser where you left them last night after your ridiculous tirade . . ." Her voice trailed off, her face strained, her brown eyes darker from fatigue, but she was still beautiful even when she was being bitchy. She had pulled up her rich, dark chocolate hair with a big barrette. Pieces of her hair had managed to escape its clasp, leaving soft, wispy curls framing her fair-skinned face, soft chin and full lips. I loved her hair that way. She wore little make up, if any at all. She was about five feet six and still taut in all the right places for a woman of forty. "Where did you go this morning?"

"My usual morning run," I stated flatly.

She picked up Ms. Levy's pamphlet. "What is this?"

"I found myself walking into her office this morning, and she handed me that brochure. She said for us to look it over, and to call, if we chose to make an appointment with her."

"Have you read it?" she curtly asked.

"No." She was picking a fight. I thought, *No more. I can't do this again with you.*

Leeta opened the flaps of the pamphlet. "Hmm, it reads:

> No one is immune to family and marital stress. Even the best of relationships has its difficulties. The stress may originate within the relationship or from the outside. However, it is the relationship that becomes endangered. The damage comes from not communicating the underlying issues, by making assumptions and drawing false conclusions. The unresolved issues fester and are compounded. The ability to resolve is lost with what had been usually very workable issues.

Leeta, her eyes laser-focused into mine, defiantly stated, "I feel we are dealing with five years of unresolved issues, and the problems are between us."

Her look was chilling. I held back. *No more fighting. What in the hell is she talking about, five years of unresolved issues? She would often say, "I couldn't be happier. We got our little patch of heaven right outside our back door." What am I missing? Apparently, a lot.*

Leeta asked, "Do you want me to continue?"

I nodded mutely, reeling from her fervor, and her comment: "five years of unresolved issues." *Our entire marriage!*

> It takes healthy persons to admit the couple or family need help with their conflicts. They are having conflict in their life-situation-complex, and they do not know what to do. Marital therapy is a process that does not tell one what to do, but offers a framework in which the couple can talk. The process's primary goal is not to judge who is right or wrong, not to take sides, but to aid the couple to come to workability in their relationships and to renew and develop their resources.

Without looking up, she continued to read from Ms. Levy's pamphlet.

> Counseling can be sought when the couple/family feel their conflict is not the norm for them and are at odds with what to do. Ideally, if this is done when the warning signs are first noted, the counseling experience can be one of personal and couple/family growth and not one of crisis intervention.

She placed the brochure back on the dresser. Her eyes were now dark and blank, as if her soul had been gutted out of her. "Have you ever been to a therapist?" Leeta asked dispassionately.

"No."

"How come?"

"It never occurred to me until now, or rather when I passed by Jane Levy's sign. Have you?"

"Chad and I went for a few sessions."

"What did you think of marriage counseling?"

"I think it would've been very worthwhile had we continued, but Chad didn't like it."

She paused and looked away. "He didn't like talking about his feelings, especially to a stranger. And he felt the therapist saw him as the bad guy, that everything was his fault."

"Oh."

We stared at each other across the space of the room, Leeta resting against the dresser absentmindedly stroking Hannah, and I still sitting on the sofa. The telephone rang. Leeta picked up the receiver.

"Hello. Yes, Kate, just a minute. It's Kate." She handed me the phone. "She wants to know if you plan to come in today."

Kate was speaking so loudly I could hear her without putting the receiver to my ear. I took the phone. "Yes,

Kate, I plan to come in. I'm leaving right now. I'll have time to prepare. Ordering the Road Warrior Sandwich and ice tea from Three Chopt would be great. Let me go, or I'll never get there."

With our silence broken, and both of us looking rather spent, I said hoarsely, "I do want our marriage to work. I do love you. I want to make an appointment with Ms. Levy. Do you?"

Leeta sighed. "Yes, I do and not just for our sake, but for Travis's. I feel so stuck with our situation. I can't stand the tension."

Chapter Three

International Commercial Insulations

"**I** WILL MAKE THE APPOINTMENT, OKAY?" I SAID, GIVING LEETA A quick kiss on the cheek, before getting into the car. Leeta leaned down and looked at me through the passenger window. "Any day after three o'clock," Leeta reminded me.

Our eyes met. "Sure," I said softly. I wanted to say something encouraging, but I just couldn't. I was completely drained from the morning's events, but at least now, I was one with the day and not detached from it. I no longer felt I was talking to someone through a wide screen, high-density television, which was exactly how I felt when I was in Ms. Levy's office, even though I clearly knew she and I were sitting in the same small waiting room across from each other. Words were coming out of my mouth, which gave me the eerie feeling it wasn't me who was actually saying them. *Please, God, I never want to feel that disturbingly weird again!*

I slowly backed up the 1966 Volvo I'd had since college and turned it around to face the driveway. I looked back toward Leeta to wave goodbye. She had already gone in, leaving Hannah sitting on the porch alone. Hannah pulled her ears back as she looked at the kitchen door and then me. "You're right, Hannah, something is wrong, very wrong at the Alfred's house," I whispered to myself.

Most mornings until early afternoon, Leeta trained her horses or others'. She didn't have a big business, but a very reputable one, producing enough income to do whatever was needed for the care of the horses. I knew nothing about horses before meeting her. I was resistant to Leeta giving me lessons, which in the beginning frustrated her to no end. "Men, they have to be so macho. Can't teach them anything, and they certainly won't ask if they need help," she retorted one afternoon, as she attempted to give me some riding hints.

I picked up a few simple horse books, took a little advice from her and found myself evolving into a weekend cowboy. She found her city boy doing quite well. Eventually, she apologized for her early remarks, "Everybody has his way to learn, and yours certainly works for you."

I released a sad sigh, remembering a more congenial and happier time together. At least the old Volvo loved me. She appreciated the time I spent with her and did not mind if I left her alone at times. She always sprang back to life when I asked her, because I always gave her what she needed. The old Volvo drove as smoothly as ever as it hugged the hairpin curve leading to the plant. She had become my trademark. Frequently, I would hear, "C.J., saw you at the City Hall meeting Thursday night till late." Or, "Did you like the play at Flat Rock Playhouse Saturday night?" I used to be taken aback when I had no recollection of the people being where I was, until they would remark, "Saw your car." As I drove through the plant's entrance, I noted the words International Commercial Insulations drawn across the length of its building. The plant's only landscaping was the woods that surrounded it.

Anything artificial would have been a distraction from nature's quiet perfection. A well-worn path through the woods had emerged from the quiet tread of those who sought solace in its tranquility and beauty. Because of Leeta's early influence, I had renewed my appreciation for what was right outside my office's door. The first time I brought her to the plant, she said, "You have your own mini Pisgah Forest, complete with its own wildlife," and pointed to the white-tailed deer, before he escaped from our view into the safety of the woods. She made me promise to do nothing to upset what was already naturally beautiful.

I parked the Volvo in the parking spot marked with my name, **C.J. Alfred, President,** in bold black letters, right beside **Kate W. Burton, Executive Manager.** To the left of Kate's was **Robert Russell, Plant Supervisor,** and beside Robert's was **David Jacobs, Sales Representative.** I walked through the side entrance that opened directly into the machine area. Machines of all sizes graced the plant's floor to make different sizes of block insulation to be put on pipefittings in seconds. Men and women of varying sizes and shapes stood beside each machine, giving a nod as I passed by. I had designed each of these machines, making the next better than its predecessor. The plant was a modest building with open spaces, buttressed by beige cinder block walls and white cement floors. Big windows along the top half of the walls let the sunshine in, giving plenty of light during the sunny days and good light on the cloudy days.

I walked through the machine room to the offices and the waiting area. Kate was waiting for me just outside her office door with my lunch. She looked at me as if trying to read my mind. "I saw you drive into the parking lot."

Kate hadn't changed a bit since I first hired her, except for the graying of her hair. "Don't worry, Kate. I'm fine."

"Good." She handed me my sandwich and ice tea from Three Chopt.

Faking an upbeat and lighthearted tone, I said, laughing nervously, "Already lunch time?"

Kate speaking in her most professional tone, "Almost, it's eleven forty-five."

Still trying to keep a lighthearted tone to deter Kate from thinking anything was wrong, I said, glancing at my watch, "What! You know me. I can lose track of time."

"No, I don't know that about you," Kate responded dispassionately. I was failing miserably. She knew me too well. "You're Mr. Punctuality." She paused and looked straight into my eyes, but I knew she wouldn't push me for any more than I wanted to give. We always maintained a very respectful co-dominate relationship. I wouldn't know what to say anyway. I was still reeling from Leeta's statement of our having five years of unresolved issues, five years . . . as long as we've been married. I was afraid too, of falling apart. I already had a really clear inkling of what it could be like to be debilitated with depression.

Her voice softened, "Do you want David and Robert in today's meeting?"

"Of course I want them in here," I responded quickly, relieved Kate had moved on with the workday's agenda. "If the New York group contracts with us, it'll be a multi-million-dollar job. I want them to feel they have a working relationship with all of us and can call whomever at any time for whatever their needs are. And Kate . . ."

"Yes."

"I'm fine."

"Good." She purposely turned away and headed for her office door.

I knew she didn't believe me. I walked into my office, sat down at my desk and began devouring my sandwich. I had forgotten I hadn't eaten breakfast and didn't realize how hungry I was until I sank my teeth into the warm, thick roast beef, honey-wheat sandwich, melt-in-your-mouth good. I kept telling myself to slow down, but couldn't. The tea was perfect, freshly brewed with just the right amount of sugar. Southern tea, nothing better.

David and Robert walked in. David was five feet seven at best, but somehow I never saw him as being a small man. Maybe it was because he was so physically fit. On the other hand, Robert was tall and angular. He had a cowlick at his hairline, which caused his sandy blond bangs to fall down onto his forehead and gave him boyish good looks, even as he neared his fiftieth birthday. They each had been with me for about fifteen years and had enjoyed the growth of the company as well as its financial growth. They, along with Kate, were major stockholders. We took care of our employees with raises and stockholder options as the company prospered, along with good medical and retirement benefits. I wanted union influence to be superfluous in my plant. I made sure the employees knew we took care of our own and well.

"Ready for today's meeting?" asked David. "Kate's been talking to herself all morning about your acting odd. Is everything okay?"

"Yes, yes to both of your questions," I retorted. Neither David nor Robert said anything. They glanced at each other quickly and sat down on the black leather couch. A deafening silence came over the room. "Are you two ready for today's contract meeting with the New York people?" I blurted out to break the stifling silence and to get everyone focused on something I could discuss.

"Don't see why we wouldn't be," answered Robert. "We've done this a hundred times before, except the money involved is more than we have ever garnished for a single job."

I breathed a sigh of relief. Back on track, and in a safe direction, away from my personal life. "Right on. If they like our product and us, there are more contracts in the offing beyond our wildest dreams."

David chuckled. "I thought that happened when we went global a few years back, having us enlarge the machine room and updating the Corporation's name from Commercial Insulations to Commercial International Insulations."

We all laughed. *Yep, this feels right. This is the world I understand and can negotiate.*

"Mr. Schwartz has arrived with his assistant," announced Kate as she entered the office. "He is not what I expected."

"What do you mean?" I asked.

"Well, I don't know exactly, but I guess I thought him being from New York City, his attire would be a dark suit."

"Oh yeah, he's not a suit man, more of a jean and shirt guy. When I met him in New York this past May, I was impressed with his casual manner. He was very easy to work with. Just didn't think to say anything to you, Kate, because jeans are standard attire here."

"But you don't wear a brown leather jacket and aviator glasses. I've never seen anybody with such blue eyes either. Just wasn't what I was expecting, that's all. Are we ready?"

"Certainly, bring them in, please."

Kate returned with George and an attractive, very young, twenty-something woman.

Wow, I thought. *What happened to Joyce? His other assistant is as drop-dead gorgeous as this one is cute.* As if he knew what I was thinking, George smiled at me directly.

"Hello C.J., good seeing you again," he said, extending his hand.

"George, good to see you too. You've met Kate already, and this is Robert Russell and David Jacobs."

"Good to meet you. This is my assistant, Corey James." She nodded her head and stood quietly beside her boss.

The meeting began with us taking a quick tour of the plant and returning to my office. The conversation flowed with Kate, Robert, David and me, attending to each detail presented by Mr. Schwartz. Corey sat quietly on the couch. Unlike Joyce, who was in lock step with George and was a strong contributor in working out the details for the New York City's contract, Corey's participation was simply being extraordinarily pleasant to look at. At the meeting's end, Kate finalized the cost of the original order, along with a speculative sheet for more insulation and its cost. It was agreed that Robert would personally supervise the installation of the first shipment to make sure everything was properly executed. David would be a telephone call away, if more materials were needed. With the meeting over and George and his assistant gone, we sat around talking about how the business had grown in the past fifteen years. We talked about the possibility of having to enlarge the plant. We certainly had the space.

"I don't know about any more enlargements," I stated. "I don't want to mess with the naturalness of this area."

"Jeez, when did this all come about?" David asked.

"Since my marriage to Leeta," I responded.

Robert clapped. "You've got my vote." This came as no surprise to me or to anyone else. Robert was an avid outdoorsman. His backyard was a safe haven for all wildlife. The whole rear of his cabin was predominately one large window with a large porch, bedecked with old heavy-duty wooden rockers. The well-published outdoorsman, Tom Brown, Jr., would definitely approve of Robert's backyard full of nature's bounty.

Kate glanced at her watch, stating it was nearing the five o'clock hour. "Anything else we need to do?"

"No, I think we covered everything. Robert and David, can you think of anything else we need to do?"

"No, think we are good to go," David replied.

Robert nodded in agreement. "Everything is signed, copied and sealed. Ready to go."

"Tomorrow bright and early," I said. Kate gave me a sideward glance. "Yes, Kate, bright and early. I'll call you if I'm not."

Everybody quietly filed out, satisfied with the day's work. Interestingly, nobody, including Kate, made a comment about George or Corey. But it was impossible not to notice their Hollywood good looks. Corey was a Kate Hudson cute, but with strawberry blond hair. And Kate was right, George had very defined blue eyes. He was almost a clone of a much younger Paul Newman, complete with his mischievous, bad boy movie persona. He had no wedding band on his finger. I did not notice whether he wore a ring when I met him in New York. I wondered what happened to Joyce, who was more age-appropriate for him than Miss Corey. Another relationship gone sour? I shuddered at the thought.

I sat down at my desk and looked around my office. My desk was big and crescent shape. My father designed it. It was big enough to contain my computer, printer and drafting board, but at the same time could serve as a conference table. I really liked it.

Pictures I photographed of the outdoors, Leeta's horses and Hannah graced my walls. The pictures I took of Leeta and Travis were on the top of the bookshelf behind my desk. I opened my side desk drawer, carefully pulled out the Hendersonville telephone book and stopped short. My eye caught an envelope addressed to me. It lay at the bottom of the drawer. I turned it on its backside and noticed the seal had been broken. I took out the folded sheet of paper and opened it wide.

In Leeta's very neat script, I read:

> *My dearest C.J.,*
> *I must write simply,*
> *For only through simplicity*
>   *can there be understanding.*
> *I must write from the heart,*
> *For only through the heart*
>   *can the truth be found.*
> *I must write to you,*
> *For only to you can I write*
>   *simply and from the heart.*
>   *I love you,*
>   *Leeta*

My breath caught in my throat. Leeta had written this when we were dating. It was the first of many poems we wrote to each other. For me, the engineer, the written word never came easy. I could draw a very lucid and meticulous picture about any idea I had, but to put my ideas in writing was an excruciating task. However, with Leeta, my words flowed from my pen like a fast-running mountain stream and in rhythmic prose, no less. When did we stop writing them? What changed between us?

I looked down at my watch and noted it was exactly five o'clock. I opened the telephone book to the yellow pages and found the listing for Marriage and Family Therapy. There was her name, **Jane H. Levy, MSW, LCSW,** in bold blue print, **N.C. Licensed Marriage and Family Therapist.** Listing her services as individual, marriage and family counseling, premarital counseling, stepfamily counseling and family and divorce mediation. *I could have used many of her services, at one time or another. I wonder why it never crossed my mind to seek help, maybe because the idea of talking to someone seemed fruitless. Why now? I'm desperate. Apparently, I didn't do such a great job with my first marriage. I'm not going to let this marriage fail.*

I picked up the phone and punched in the telephone numbers. My hand was shaking. Her answering machine picked up, saying, "Hello, this is the office of Jane Levy. I'm either with a client or away from the phone. Please leave a message after the beep. Take as much time as you need. Be sure to repeat your name and number, as your message is important to me. I will call you back as soon as possible. If this is an emergency, please call 911. Thanks and have a great day."

Well, her voice sounds friendly enough. Calming, in fact. "Yes, this is C.J. Alfred. I met you this morning in your office. You gave me one of your brochures. My wife and I would like to make an appointment with you. You may call me either at work today or tomorrow until six o'clock at 555-5432 or at home 555-5845. Thank you."

I released my breath, which I hadn't realized I'd been holding. So much for my legendary calm. Apparently, brokering a multimillion dollar deal didn't faze me, but one measly call to a counselor, and I'm breaking into a sweat. I looked out the large picture window above the bookshelf. It was almost twilight. The last of the sun's rays were peeking through the trees.

The phone rang, "Hello, C.J. Alfred speaking."

"Yes, Jane Levy, returning your call for an appointment . . ."

"Yes, any time after three o'clock will do."

"Would next Tuesday at four o'clock work for you?"

I looked at my calendar. "Tuesday's clear, nothing is scheduled."

"And your wife's name?"

"Leeta."

"Good, you know where my office is?"

"Yes, office in back."

"Correct. I look forward to meeting with the two of you. Please call me, if there is a conflict with the appointment."

"I sure will."

"Thank you. Good bye."

"Good bye." I put down the phone and breathed deeply. Once again, my hands were shaking and sweaty. *I hope this gets easier,* I thought. I wrote in my calendar, Tuesday at 4:00, office in back. I turned around and looked at the smiling faces of Leeta and Travis. *I don't want to lose them. Travis, even though he is my stepson, I feel he is my son. I love that boy, not only that, I like him. He is as important to me as Leeta is. Tuesday at 4:00. Office in back. We'll be there.*

Chapter Four

Tuesday at Four

TUESDAY SOON ARRIVED. I WAS AT THE HOUSE PROMPTLY AT three-thirty. Travis was already home from school, standing on the porch when I drove up the drive. "So, this is the big day," he said as I got out of the Volvo and walked to the front door.

"Yep, sure is."

"Are you scared?"

"Scared, well, I don't know." Feigning cool, I continued, "Your mother and I are hopeful this will help us have a better relationship. We know we love each other. We just need some help in working out a few things." I lied. I was scared.

"I hope so. I don't understand all this stuff about adults loving each other. Mom said she loved Dad, but they weren't happy together. I don't get it."

Leeta walked out onto the porch just when Travis finished stating his confusion. We looked at each other. *This sure as hell isn't my place to say anything,* I thought.

"I understand your feelings, Travis." Leeta finally spoke. "I told you, your dad and I married too young. We didn't know each other, much less ourselves, well enough to get married. We realized over the years we were too different in what we wanted as a couple."

"Yes, I remember you telling me that. But you said with C.J., you not only loved him, but you two had a lot in common," Travis said with an edge in his voice.

"Yes," Leeta said slowly, "that is what I said. That's why we've made this appointment with Ms. Levy. We both want this marriage to work because of that."

Mother and son stood looking at each other, and this time Travis broke the silence. "Good luck, you guys," he said. He kissed his mother, and walked over to hug me. Damn, I was again straining to fight back those now all-too-familiar, out-of-control emotions, which were exploding in the back of my throat and threatening this time, to choke me for sure.

Leeta and I walked to the Volvo together, and I opened the passenger door for her. Leeta whispered, "Been a long time since you've opened a door for me, C.J. Most of the time you're walking twenty feet ahead of me."

Jeez, I thought. Woman, what will it take to please you? Always a criticism, never any appreciation for what I do. I'm trying here. I walked around to the driver's side, got in, looked straight ahead and saw Travis still standing on the front porch with Hannah sitting by his side. Hannah was always there when needed, the built-in radar that "man's best friend" is noted for. And if anybody needed a friend, it was Travis. Never did a kid look so alone. As I turned to look over my right shoulder to back the Volvo, Leeta with trembling lips, was blowing Travis a kiss.

We drove the few blocks to Jane Levy's office in quiet, and continued to do so as we entered her office. As we sat down, I could hear a muffled female voice talking, and then silence. Ms. Levy came from a side room and stood at the waiting room door. "Hello, Mr. Alfred and Mrs. Alfred," she said, smiling warmly and extending her hand toward Leeta to shake and then me. She shook my hand with a firm grip as she had done with Leeta. She invited us into the room she came out of when I first met her. "In here please, this is the room where we'll have our sessions. Please be seated in these two chairs."

The room was pleasant with three comfortable chairs surrounding a low table that had a box of tissue, two yellow pads and a hand-painted dish with a couple of ink pens resting in it. A lamp, a small antique clock and an old phone with a rotary dial sat on a small side table against the left wall. I wondered if it worked. On the right wall were diplomas from the University of Georgia and North Carolina at Chapel Hill, along with NC state board licenses in clinical social work and marriage and family therapy. A picture of a pretty, teen-age girl smiled at us from the bookshelf on the back wall. I wondered if this was her daughter.

I waited for Leeta to choose where she wanted to sit. She looked at me as if to ask if I had a preference. I smiled and opened my arms suggesting it didn't matter. *Will we ever feel normal around each other again?* I mused. When we finally sat down, Jane sat in a chair that faced ours. She looked at Leeta and asked, "Your name is Leeta?"

"Yes," said Leeta.

"It's a lovely name. Mr. Alfred, you are called by your initials, and not by another name?"

"Yes."

"My name is Jane. I usually refer to my clients on a first name basis. Is this okay with you?" We both nodded. It sounded good to me, anything to get things more relaxed.

Then Jane Levy quickly went over some paperwork regarding birthdates, mailing address, telephone numbers and fee. "Are you comfortable with the fee?" Jane asked.

"For me, your fee is a small price to pay if you can help us," I said, looking over at Leeta.

Leeta nodded.

"I hope to do just that, but I can't do it without your help. I need you to work with me as much as you need me to work with you. Today, what I need is your educating me about you. I'll be as good as the information you give me." Jane paused. "Any questions so far?"

We both shook our heads. Leeta sat with her back straight, rigidly poised on the edge of her chair with both hands in her lap. She reminded me of the assiduous college girl, taking in every word of her professor, not a point missed, lest it showed up on the next exam.

"Okay then. I'm going to ask you each three questions, the same three questions. The choice of who begins is up to the two of you. Whoever starts has the blessing of getting it over with, and the burden of initiating everything."

"And if you begin second?" I asked.

"The blessing of listening to what the first person initiates, and the burden of not responding in defense to the first person's responses. I want to know your issues exactly as you need me to understand them; not whether or not you agree or disagree with your partner. Am I making myself clear?"

"I understand," Leeta responded, still perched on the edge of her seat.

Jeez, woman, relax. "Yes," I responded.

"If you choose to continue counseling with me and I with you, you'll have all the time you need and want to share your opinions. Are there any questions?"

"If we choose to continue with you?" Leeta asked. Her hands now were clutched so tight her knuckles looked like little white knobs sitting on top of her curled fingers.

"Yes, if you decide to make another appointment with me. It's important we're comfortable with each other. Let's begin with both of you taking a deep breath and sitting back in your chairs."

Leeta sat back and took a deep breath, as I did too. I had not noticed how comfortable my chair was until I felt myself sink into its cushiony splendor. I, also, had been sitting on the edge of my seat. "This chair feels great!" I exclaimed, patting both armrests.

"Good, that's exactly what I wanted for my clients— big comfortable chairs. Now, who would like to begin?" Jane asked with a smile as she looked at both of us.

"It doesn't matter to me who begins," I said. "Do you want to start, Leeta?"

"It doesn't matter," Leeta replied, shrugging her shoulders. She had at least unclenched her hands as they now rested easily on her chair's armrests. She was still very erect in her chair but had sat back into it.

"Then I guess I will," I said, positioning myself more securely into my chair.

"Well then." Jane picked up one of the yellow pads off the table in front of us. "What changed that made you decide to phone and include someone like me into your life?"

"What changed?" I asked uncertainly. I thought, *We need help. Is that the answer, she is looking for? That should be obvious.*

Jane continued, "Yes, what changed? Generally, my experience of working with couples is them bringing in problems they have been dealing with for some time. My only hope is that couples come in before the energy of the heart burns out. Yes, what changed that you felt talking to a therapist might help?"

"The fighting," I replied. "The fighting became more frequent and could last way into the night. We kept fighting about the same things. Many times I couldn't remember what started the fighting in the first place, but I did remember the mean words. We both would apologize a few days later about what we said to each other, but . . ."

"Yes?" Jane asked.

"I guess the only thing positive about the fighting was the make-up times, but that's not even happening now." I stopped abruptly.

"Is there more?" Jane asked as she ceased writing on her note pad. I had never seen anyone write as fast as she did. I wondered if she was taking her notes in some form of short hand or code.

"This makes my second marriage. I was married the first time for ten years to my college girlfriend. I married her because I loved her and because I wanted to live the rest of my life with her. Then we just grew apart. We were more like roommates by the end of our marriage. I fell in love a second time with Leeta, and we got married. I don't want to lose Leeta. I'm fearful I will unless something changes."

"If I understand you correctly, the reason you're seeking marriage counseling is because of yours and Leeta's frequent fighting with harsh and painful words. Seldom do you feel you two work anything out, much less remember what starts the fight in the first place. Now you're fearful this marriage will end in divorce like your first marriage. Did I understand you correctly?"

Hearing her repeat back what I said so compactly gave a power punch to my gut. I grimaced with the unambiguous harshness of her rephrase. "Yes, that's what I said," I confirmed reluctantly.

"Is there more?"

"That's all I can think of for right now?"

"The second question is, what significant information do I need to work with you? Remember, I'll be only as good as the information you give me."

"Whew, that's a good one. I'll try. I'm apparently not meeting Leeta's needs. As I understand it, she tells me we don't spend enough quality time together. However, I feel we do.

"Leeta and I have a difference of opinion on what is neatness. She tells me I clutter up the house with my stuff and overfill the bookshelves with all my books. I, on the other hand, feel it is okay for a home to have that lived-in looked. She gets upset with Travis and me if we leave an empty glass on a side table in the family room. We have to take our shoes off and leave them in the mudroom before entering the house. I cannot lie on the bed with my work clothes on. I can't enjoy a Sunday morning, reading the Sunday papers, without Leeta getting so obsessive with getting the house picked up before leaving for church. Frequently, she throws the newspapers into the recycle bin before I have a chance to read them. It's the only time of the week I feel I have the time to read them in their entirety.

"Listening to my telling you this stuff, it seems so silly. Is this why we're here? Fighting over when the Sunday papers get picked up and thrown away? This is embarrassing."

Looking up from her note taking, Jane stated, "Don't be. It's the 'silly' stuff that can destroy the love couples have for each other."

"So the silly stuff isn't so silly?"

"Absolutely not," she responded emphatically. "This silly stuff is actually your dailiness with each other, how you live together day by day. Is there more?"

I cleared my throat. "Well, there is more of this silly stuff, but this is enough for now."

"Okay then, the third question," Jane continued, looking straight at me. "What do you want to accomplish in counseling? What are your goals?"

"To get back to the way things used to be with us and to learn how to deal with this silly stuff, so we don't destroy our love for each other. To communicate better and to stop fighting; the fighting has to stop."

"Thank you for the information," Jane responded, and turned her attention to Leeta. "Now the same three questions for you. What changed?"

Leeta didn't hesitate to answer. In fact, her words shot out of her mouth like a rapid-firing Gatling gun. "Yes, what changed?

"The fighting that has no resolutions. The fighting that gets meaner and louder. You know that old saying, 'sticks and stones can break your bones, but words can never hurt you.' That's a lie. They do, and they go right to your soul. And if repeated enough, you begin to wonder if they're true. Saying you were angry and didn't mean what you said just doesn't fly anymore.

"My not liking who I'm becoming being married to C.J. Or what I'm teaching my child, Travis, about love and marriage—that the two go together like oil and water, not horse and carriage."

Leeta finally stopped, thank goodness. She was leaning forward again with her hands clenched so tightly that the little white knobs on top of her tight curled fingers had reappeared. *It was a mistake coming here,* I reflected. *Jane Levy is stirring everything up with her questions. Damn it, I should have known this was going to happen. Why didn't I think to meet Leeta here, instead of picking her up in the Volvo? At least, I would have escaped the firestorm on the way home.*

"Okay," Jane responded calmly, slowing Leeta's rapid discharge. "You, as well, want to have a better way of communicating other than the mean loud fighting and are tired of having the fights with no resolutions. You also don't like who you're becoming with C.J., and what you're teaching Travis. Is that correct?"

"That's correct. But our fighting is not the only breakdown in our communication. I'm not getting what I need from him because I guess I don't communicate to C.J. in an understandable manner. He never seems to get it."

Because I feel like I'm getting shot at from a mouth that shoots bullets, I thought.

"So you don't feel you're communicating to C.J. in an understandable manner?" Jane queried.

"Yes. He can't see the bigger picture because apparently my examples don't make sense to him."

"I don't understand. Say it another way?" Jane queried again.

"For example, his forgetting to take out the trash—the bigger picture is reliability. Can I really depend on him? Or my asking him to cut the Christmas ham and two hours later it still hasn't been carved. The carving of the ham is not the issue, but reliability and my feeling my needs are unimportant. Then I break down and become this very unattractive person whom I don't even like or want to be with. He just doesn't get it."

"So the breakdown of your communication with each other is more than the fighting. It's not being understood in the way you want to be understood. Also you're wondering whether your needs are important to him."

"Yes. Finally, I'm understood by at least someone," Leeta stated with the emphasis on finally.

Ah shit, I thought. *Reliability, what in the hell is she talking about. She hasn't had it so good since she married me.* I could feel my muscles tighten in my neck and chest. I wanted to walk out. *How much longer can I sit in this room with these women, listening to the C.J. bash fest?*

"Okay then, what's the significant information that I need to most effectively work with you two?"

"My growing resentment toward C.J. He's always finding time to be with his employees, but not with me or Travis. We're last on his to-do list. Asking me to meet him downtown for lunch happens rarely, and if he does invite me, something frequently comes up that he can't go. His employees are more family to him than we are. They're always having lunch together. A 'honey-do' list being done for me—in my dreams. He's happy as can be working on his Volvo, and he can spend more time and passion 'doing copy' on his ham radio than with me." Leeta paused.

Her eyes darkened and her jaw line tightened.

She looked directly toward me, but through me at the same time. *That's a look I've seen way too many times recently.*

"I pick at him over the little things that really mean nothing to me. I feel if I'm going to be miserable, then he is too. Sounds sick, doesn't it?" Leeta asked flatly.

Jane answered softly, "No, it doesn't."

"I married C.J. to have someone to share my life. I didn't marry C.J. to be alone. I did that quite successfully unmarried. Now being married to C.J., I'm still alone and worse yet, I'm lonely." Leeta's voice broke as tears streamed down her face.

"C.J., please hand Leeta the box of tissue," Jane said quietly.

Jeez, I thought as I handed the tissues to Leeta. *You're lonely being married to me? Lonely?*

"Please continue," Jane said. "Don't let your tears stop you. They are important too."

"Sometimes I feel I married the same man again. Once again, I'm on the bottom of my husband's priority list. The only difference is with my first husband, Chad, I competed with his hunting schedule and poker night." Leeta paused and looked at me now with dark brooding eyes, her face flushed. Wisps of her hair had now fallen from the big barrette that pulled her hair up to the crown of her head and off her neck.

"C.J. is getting upset," Leeta said.

"That true?" Jane asked, turning her attention to me.

"Yes, so I'm the bad guy? Do I do anything to satisfy you?"

"I didn't hear Leeta call you a bad guy," Jane interjected. "If anything, I heard Leeta say she felt herself to be the 'bad guy' in her growing resentment toward you and her picking at you to make you as miserable as she feels."

"Well, I sure as hell haven't heard her say anything she liked about me." I said curtly.

"I'm hearing her share her issues of concern as you did. By the way, there are no bad guys here. You both have participated in the failures of this marriage. As you both will participate in the successes of this marriage," Jane said firmly.

Jane, turning her attention back to Leeta asked, "Are you okay?"

"I guess."

"Is there more you would like to share?"

There's more? I screamed to myself. *You're too high maintenance for me, lady.* The muscles in my neck were tightening more. My head was pounding. *What is the point of us being in counseling anyway? You're married to a man who does nothing for you.*

Leeta said slowly, "Yes, there's more. I'm having the same fights I had with my first husband that I'm now having with C.J. It's his time spent away from home with friends, colleagues or when home with hobbies. It's the untidiness as it was with Chad, especially after I've spent all day cleaning house. It's needed repairs around the house that get put off even after promises made. It's when to have sex, or not enough sex. These are the ones that come to mind first.

"And there are differences too, good differences," Leeta continued. "C.J. is more connected to Travis than Chad ever was and is. He is good to my parents and welcomes them to our home and joins me graciously on special family occasions. Money is not a huge issue with us as it was in my first marriage. I don't worry about the heat being cut off because of the bill that allegedly was paid and really wasn't. I trust C.J. I don't feel he keeps things from me. And I do love him."

So I do something right, I mused.

"Is there more?" Jane asked.

"No more."

About time, I thought. I could feel my damp shirt sticking to my skin. My head hurt so bad I felt I was going to puke. I looked down at my watch, four-fifty. Ten more minutes before the session was up. God, if there was any way I could leave, I would.

Jane now turning her attention to me asked, "How are you doing?"

"Not so good," I responded.

"You're normal. First sessions are difficult."

I thought, *Normal, I sure don't feel normal.* Second sessions are not difficult? I wondered if anyone noticed my shirt was becoming damp with perspiration and yes, in the most embarrassing areas.

"We have about ten minutes left in the session, and I want to ask Leeta the third question, goals . . . what are your goals?"

"Goals," Leeta responded slowly and turned toward me. "Are we looking for the same things in a marriage? This is scary for me to say. Things that are really important to me in a relationship, I fear aren't for you. I want us to share more things together than we do now. This is a real deal-breaker for me, if we cannot work this out. Yes, you've learned to ride, and a natural at that. Yes, we've ridden on weekends, but only if you have nothing else on your schedule. Yes, we've worked together as a family training Hannah. But generally, what you consider quality time together, I don't. Yes, I want you to have your independence with your friends and hobbies, but this I feel is too much at the expense of our relationship. Yes, I feel since we've been married I've been added on your 'to-do' list, but at the bottom. Can we work this out? That's my goal. And of course, I want us to communicate better. The fighting has to stop."

"Thank you," Jane said. "Thank you both. I know this has been a difficult session for you both, but I do want you to know, the sessions early in the counseling process can be difficult because of the emotional rawness of the issues."

Difficult doesn't describe it, I thought. *My head is pounding.*

"Our time is almost up. The decision now is whether you two want to schedule another appointment. There's nothing presented today that alarms me. This is not to make light of your issues, but to say you're normal. These issues are inherent to some degree in any marriage. You can't escape them."

"So we're a normal married couple dealing with normal stuff," I said incredulously.

"Yes," Jane replied with a smile. "You're a normal couple dealing with very normal issues and concerns. I call them living issues."

I looked over at Leeta. Those brown eyes of hers now had some degree of life in them.

"Yes," Jane replied again. "The easy part of any relationship is the falling in love part. The hard part is learning how to live with each other under the same roof. Do you want to make another appointment?"

Leeta said softly, "I do."

You do, with what you don't like about me? I thought. *I don't know if I can ever make you happy.* Then I heard me say, "Me too."

"Good." Jane smiled. "Now you have a homework assignment," she firmly stated.

Homework! What! I gasped to myself.

"That is for you two not to discuss any of the issues that were presented today. You've already told me you don't do this very well."

"Got that one right," I blurted out.

Jane continued, "You both said you have the energy of the heart. I call that the 'gasoline' to do the work needed to repair the relationship."

"'The energy of the heart,' you mean we still love each other?" Leeta asked.

"That's what I heard both of you say, correct?"

We both nodded our heads. However, I doubted whether I could meet Leeta's expectations of her dream man.

"Excellent, that's the main ingredient needed for me to work with you two. I've got to have the desire, the energy of the heart, and without that, it doesn't matter how hard I work with you, I'll not be effective."

"And the other assignment is to have fun, to remind each other why you got married in the first place. I assume this is one of the reasons why you got married, you had fun?"

"Yes, we used to have fun, lots of fun," Leeta said quietly.

"Yes, we did." I agreed. *It has been a long time, too long,* I thought.

*　*　*

Leeta and I were quiet on the drive home. Travis met us at the kitchen door with Hannah at his side, wagging her tail and a toy in her mouth.

"Well?" He asked impatiently.

"Well," Leeta said hesitantly as she reached for her son's face with both hands and kissed him. "We're a normal couple with normal living issues."

"Huh? And that means?" Travis asked as he eased away from Leeta's hold and looked at us with the same deep brown eyes of his mother's.

"That means our issues are what every couple deals with in making a life together, and with hard work we'll work all of our issues out."

"When we do our homework this week, we are to have fun," I said.

"Yes," Leeta said cautiously, as she looked at me and then Travis, "to have fun as a couple and a family."

* * *

Leeta was already in bed lying on her side. Her soft, dark, chocolate brown curls slipped down over her shoulders and almost hid her face. I wanted so badly to brush them away and kiss her soft, full lips, but there was no gesture from her that this would be okay.

Standing in front of the bathroom mirror while I brushed my teeth, I noticed I looked old, way beyond my forty-seven years. Dark circles framed my eyes, and deep wrinkles stretched across my forehead. My gray eyes stared back at me . . . empty. I couldn't stop thinking about the session we had with Jane and what Leeta had said. I knew our relationship was precarious, but hearing it directly from Leeta somehow made it so much more real. I couldn't stop thinking about her saying she felt she married the same man again and asking whether we were looking for the same thing in a marriage. The kicker was her being lonely married to me. I winced with that thought. These words haunted me, and I knew why. Cullen said those exact words to me, but I thought Cullen was selfish. I blamed her for not understanding that my time spent at work was for us to have a better life one day.

When I finally got into bed, Leeta was curled up tight on her side of the bed, a scenario that had become way too familiar. I lay on my side of the bed, careful not to touch her. I looked obsessively at the clock, hoping the minute hand would move faster. Midnight, twelve-twenty, one o'clock, one-thirty. *God, I can't stand this, another long night. Do I get up? That's what they say you should do when you can't sleep.* However, when I had done this, I was up for the rest of the night. But at least, I had the comfort of Hannah lying at my feet.

I sighed. I rolled over to look at the clock. Only two o'clock. I rolled over toward Leeta. She was in the same curled up position except tighter. I missed those nights I pulled her close and she folded into me perfectly. I missed feeling her heart beating and hearing her slow easy breathing. She was the only sleep aid I needed to get a good night's sleep.

I sighed. I rolled over to look at the clock, only five minutes had passed. I felt Hannah's soft nose pressing against my back. I rolled over again and saw Hannah staring at me with her muzzle resting on the bed.

"You up too, girl?" I whispered, easing myself out of the bed, grabbing my bathrobe off the rack inside the closet door and slipping my feet inside my slippers. "Come girl," I said quietly.

I eased open the front door and sat down on one of the sturdy, wood rocking chairs, which graced our porch. I closed my eyes, rocking easily, taking in the smells of an autumn complete with the residual smell of burnt wood from the kitchen wood stove. Hannah lay at my feet with her ball in her mouth. I could hear the horses' quiet neighing in the pasture.

I closed my eyes with a heavy sigh. Flashed through my mind were memories of long ago on another fall evening as I kissed Cullen under every lamppost to her dorm.

We married the summer after we both graduated from college. On our wedding day, I could not have been happier saying, "I do," to this perky, cleft-chinned girl with the turned-up nose. She wore a simple white, cotton gown and flowers in her hair. I remembered her blond hair shone like gold in the summer sun. I swallowed hard as I remembered her whispering into my ear, "I will always love you, C.J., forever and a day." I touched my cheek as I remembered the tender brush of her lips against my face. John Denver's song about his wife, Annie, became my song, as it defined so completely my love for Cullen, my bride, my wife. His lyrics, "she fills up my senses," I hummed constantly in the early years of our marriage. The year Cullen and I divorced, I read in the paper that John and Annie

Denver were divorcing. "We just grew apart," was his only explanation. It was mine too. Hannah nudged my hand, and I was jolted awake. When did I fall asleep? I looked at the sky that was still pitch black with bright stars strewn over its broad expanse and a bright full moon topping the tree line.

"Come on, girl, let's go upstairs." I wearily lay down on top of the bed covers and turned my head to look at the clock on the bedside table. Five-ten. Jeez, I had been on the porch for over three hours. Five twenty-five, the alarm clock sounded out its tune, and as it did, Leeta reached out and touched my hand.

"You didn't sleep well last night, did you?"

I whispered, "No, did you?"

"Off and on. Where did you go?"

"I sat on the porch, and I must have fallen asleep."

"Hmm, country breakfast when you get back from your run?" she asked.

"A big breakfast on a weekday?"

"We're to have fun, remember?" Leeta said hesitantly.

"You're on," I said, getting out of bed. I dressed, tied up my running shoes and grabbed my hooded jacket. "Are you sure about the big breakfast? Don't you want to sleep instead?"

"No," Leeta responded quietly.

In the kitchen, Hannah was already waiting with her ball in tow and wagging her tail.

"Wanna go for a run, girl?"

Hannah dropped her ball and barked. "Shh, girl, you'll wake Travis," I said as I took her lead from the kitchen pantry door and attached it to her collar.

Out the door and down the long, dirt drive we went. We turned left from the driveway onto familiar streets and passed time-honored homes of yesteryear and the old oak tree that was still full of its fall leaves. The moon was out, and the stars still lit the early morning fall sky. I looked down at my watch, five forty-five. There were only a few cars out. The morning rush hadn't begun. I looked over at Hannah. Her tail hadn't stopped wagging. If there was anything this dog loved to do more than play fetch, it was to run. Lately, I hadn't had the presence of mind to invite her.

The run relaxed me. The cool breeze against my face was invigorating. *Yes, yes,* I thought, *Ms. Levy did say we were a normal couple with normal issues. And yes, that we do love each other.* Hannah and I turned the corner. We ran down Sixth. We passed Ms. Levy's sign and the bold letters, **Office in Back**. How many times had I passed this sign and never noticed it? Now I couldn't miss it.

Our homework assignment was to have fun. We could do that. We used to do it well: the evenings we sat in the kitchen, drinking coffee and eating hot brownies just out of the oven; the hours we sat on the couch just kissing; the day trips and hikes we took during the week while Travis was in school. We found ourselves enjoying the beautiful and isolated mountain views, streams and waterfalls. I took pictures, and Leeta became my favorite subject with the Blue Ridge Mountains as a backdrop. On warm days, she often took off her clothes, as if she wanted nothing to interfere with the natural lushness that surrounded her. She was so comfortable in her own skin and taught me how to do the same. We talked like I never talked to anyone before. My dark thoughts of yesterday's session were breaking up. I felt my face soften as I remembered our good times.

When did all of that stop? I slowed to a halt and bent over, placing my hands on my thighs. *When? Why?* I could feel the dread that had been filling my gut for months now recur. I sat down on the curb. The anguish I was feeling took my breath. I've never felt such sorrowful pain. Hannah sat beside me quietly. I wrapped my arm around her shoulder and brought her close to me. She rested her head easily on my shoulder. Her large, warm presence was comforting and safe feeling. I took a deep breath. I stood up and raised my fist to the sky. "I'm ready," I declared aloud. Hannah barked and bounded up with me. She wagged her tail furiously, jumping in front of me with a loud bark. "Yes, Hannah, I'm ready," I said, softly rubbing her silky head. "Fun we can do, and we do have the 'gasoline.'" I took another deep breath and exhaled strongly, hoping to release the tight coils of tension circling my heart. The morning sky was turning pink at its edges, just before the morning sun began to show its face. We ran down Short Street and then down the driveway to the house, and I smelled the bacon.

Chapter Five
Why Did We Marry?

JANE ASKED, "HOW WAS YOUR WEEK, LEETA?"
"Good," Leeta responded, looking at me.

"What changed?" Jane continued.

"Hmm, what changed?" Leeta paused. "Well, your homework assignments were for us to have fun with each other and not to discuss any of the issues. And that's what we did."

"And you?" Jane asked, turning her attention to me.

I responded, "The same. We've had a good week, so much so it seems strange we need to see you."

"We had a good week because we didn't talk about our issues," Leeta sneered. "Nothing's been worked out! God, that's what you do, C.J., try to ignore everything, just don't talk about anything, then everything is fine."

I was stunned. She popped like she had just touched a hot pan."

"All right now," Jane interrupted. "Both of you take a deep breath."

"A deep breath?" Leeta asked incredulously. Leeta turned and faced me. Her color had completely drained from her face, and two very empty, dark abysses stared at me.

"Yes," Jane responded with a smile, "like counting to ten to calm down. Follow my directives, please, by first closing your eyes."

I would do anything to make right what just exploded or emptied inside of Leeta. We both closed our eyes.

"Good, eyes closed, sitting in the comfortable chairs beside each other, take a deep breath in and notice what your body feels like each time your chest falls. Notice your body becoming quieter and quieter, calmer and calmer . . . and breathe one more time for good measure and open your eyes when you're ready."

I glanced at the table clock. It was four twenty! I thought we'd been breathing only for a few minutes, not twenty. The breathing did prevent my neck muscles from tightening and my skin from breaking out in a sweat. The color had returned to Leeta's face. *Thank you, Ms. Levy.*

"The homework did exactly what I had hoped. You reminded each other why you got married in the first place, correct?"

"Well." Leeta looked down and then at Jane. "If you had asked me that question last week, I probably couldn't answer it. Yes, your assignment worked.

"So why did you marry C.J.?" Jane asked.

Leeta closed her eyes and sighed. She seemed to take forever to respond. "First, I love how C.J. looks," she stated slowly as a slight smile spread across her face, "His lean body, his square jaw, the way he looks out of his eyes . . ."

"Yes," Jane coaxed.

"And," Leeta continued thoughtfully, "we enjoy similar things and simple things, a hike in the forest or sitting at the kitchen table enjoying a cup of coffee together. He is good with Travis, and Travis likes him. C.J. has a quirky sense of humor that most of the time makes me laugh, sometimes not. He supports me in pursuing my work with horses and takes an interest in them himself. He probably now has a whole bookshelf devoted to horses. He's not afraid to take risks in pursuing his own dreams, but isn't stupid with them either. He's honest and fair. I don't know. He's just a good man."

Well, a lot different from last week, I mused. *We did have a great week, so why the big bug-a-boo earlier?*

Jane finished jotting down Leeta's last remarks, turned her attention toward me and asked, "And you?"

"Let me see, so why did I marry Leeta? I can honestly say love at first sight. She is beautiful . . . and independent; she took care of herself and her son for several years, and did this well. She gave me a family, not just a son but also horses and now a dog. Leeta was correct when she said we enjoy similar and simple things, but she reintroduced them to me. She reminded me to notice and appreciate what was around me, like a crisp fall day. I had forgotten to enjoy them and didn't even recognize that was what I'd done. It was work, home and back to work again."

Jane stopped her note taking and looked at both of us. "So, you two married each other for the right reasons. You love, enjoy and enhance each other."

"Yes, I think so."

Leeta didn't comment, and for me, her silence was penetrating.

Jane assuaged the silence. "I'm a firm believer that most couples marry each other for the right reasons, that they love and have fun with each other, have a lot in common and enough difference to learn from. So then the question is asked, 'How come one out of two marriages ends in divorce?'" Jane looked squarely at both of us.

Good question, I thought. *Until now, I always assumed people just made a mistake and married the wrong person. That's what I had concluded when my marriage to Cullen failed.* A panic-like surge ran from my heart to the pit of my stomach. *Was Leeta thinking she just made a mistake?*

"Or do you disagree and think fifty percent of the marriages fail because we simply made a mistake in our choice of whom we chose to marry?"

God, she's reading my mind?

"I don't know." Leeta responded. "I thought I married C.J. for the right reasons, and that he was my soul mate. I'm really confused now because so many of our fights are so similar to my fights with Chad."

"What would you say if I said the reason your fights with Chad and now C.J. are so similar is because you are in a relationship."

"My fights are so similar because I'm in a relationship?" Leeta echoed.

"Yes, but let me begin by explaining why we're attracted to one another and not someone else. The relationship theory states we're attracted to each other initially because we like what we see, each other's physicality. Leeta, you noted your attraction to C.J.'s lean body, square jaw line and the way he looked out of his eyes. Right?"

"Yes," Leeta replied quietly.

Jane continued, "And C.J., you found Leeta beautiful?"

"Correct, she is beautiful to me."

"Good point," Jane continued. "She is beautiful to you, or 'beauty is in the eye of the beholder.' You match physically. You're both tall and lean. You fit. With the couple that doesn't fit, my antenna goes up a notch. It does make me wonder if they married for the right reason. Or what has changed with the relationship or with the individual that they no longer match physically. Are you with me so far?"

We nodded. *Interesting,* I reflected, *I met Leeta at a New Year's party. I almost didn't go, never been one for parties, especially New Year's. They always start late, along with the unspoken rules that guests were to stay until midnight and to kiss somebody. I didn't have anybody to kiss. Awkward was my only feeling that night.*

The small house was dim and jam-packed with people. I could barely move. I could feel my heart pounding as my memories of Leeta became more vivid. But of all those people, she stood out. To me, she was beautiful.

"Yes?" Asked Jane.

"Huh?" I responded.

"And you're thinking?"

"About what you were just saying about 'beauty in the eyes of the beholder.' I was attracted to Leeta immediately. We were in a room full of people, and she was the only one I noticed. I didn't tell Leeta then, not until I proposed to her over two years later, that I knew she was the woman I wanted to marry months into our dating."

"Uh huh, but more is needed other than being attracted to one's physical appearance," Jane stated, "and that is what comes out of our mouths. Do you know what I mean?"

"Think so," answered Leeta. "C.J. and I only met briefly that night because I was with someone else. We again met by accident, a few weeks later downtown. I was looking for a friend's birthday gift at Narnia Studios on Main Street. C.J. invited me for coffee in a nearby café. We probably talked for hours, but it felt like minutes. I never felt so comfortable with a person that I knew for such a short period."

"So you liked what came out of each other's mouths?"

"I don't know exactly," Leeta said hesitantly. "C.J. is so easy to talk with when he wants to be. We seem to agree on a lot on issues. He is so supportive of my goals and me. I don't know. From the beginning, we just seemed to click. But after we got married, that connection that was so easy, now seems so hard."

The connection that seemed so easy stopped. I winced. I'd heard this before from Cullen. I could feel the back of my shirt sticking to my skin again as the uninvited memories rushed in.

"You just don't get it," Cullen had said. "What you do and what you decide affects me. Your fears, your joys, your frustrations affect me. You can't exclude me and say it's none of my business, not my problem. It *is* my problem, just like it's your problem."

"Yes?" Jane asked, firmly looking directly at me. "Your thoughts?"

"Leeta saying, 'The connection that was so easy, now has stopped.'"

"I didn't hear Leeta say that, Leeta?" Jane asked.

"No, I said the connection between us that was so easy, now seems so hard."

"C.J., what did you hear Leeta say?"

"The connection that was so easy now seems so hard."

Jane said slowly, "Not stopped . . ."

"Yes," I said. "Not stopped." I couldn't think now. I could feel the heat rise from my chest and into my face. I was on fire.

"Are you okay?" Jane asked softly.

"No, I'm not okay."

"What's happening?"

"I've heard this before, or very similar to what Leeta's saying, but in another relationship."

"With your first wife?"

"Yes."

"Hmm."

"Hmm, what?" I said agitatedly.

"Like I've already said, I believe people marry each other for the right reasons. They love each other, have fun together, a lot in common and just enough difference to learn from, but still one out of two marriages ends in divorce."

"How come?" I asked.

"Couples choose not to negotiate out the balance needed, in order to live with each other. That's the hard part. I've always said marriages are made in heaven; staying there takes work."

"Balance?"

"Yes, reaching a balance in the living issues that are inherent in every successful marriage. We'll get more into living issues in our next session. But the good news is, you two did marry the right person. I want you two to continue to work on strengthening your desire, the energy of the heart. That's the gasoline I need in order to work with you. So your homework assignment is still to have fun and not talk about the issues. Agree?"

"Agree," I said relieved.

"Leeta?" Jane asked.

"Agree, as long as C.J. understands that because we have fun doesn't mean that the marriage is fixed."

"Yes, I understand loud and clear," I responded, clipping my words.

* * *

Once again, Leeta and I drove home in silence. The house was a welcome sight. Hannah already stood outside the Volvo's passenger door, waiting for Leeta to get out. The house smelled of chili that Leeta had slow cooked all day. The baked rice and the cornbread wrapped in foil were ready to be taken out of the oven and devoured. The table was set, inviting everyone to come and eat. But most of all, thank heaven, Travis made the dinnertime easy as he chatted about school projects due and his wanting to go to the Friday night homecoming football game.

As Travis and I were clearing the dinner dishes off the table, I asked. "Travis, have you finished your homework?"

"Almost, why?"

"Well, we've got about an hour and a half of good sunlight left. Thought you might want to help me replace the fuel pump to the Volvo. The old pump has been acting up lately. I bought a new pump the other day at Arnold's and I've just been waiting for a time for us to get together. You up for it?"

"Sure am!" exclaimed Travis.

Leeta smiled and nodded her head. "I'll school Ajax while you two work on the car."

Travis and I walked toward the converted carriage house garage. "Do you want to be primary mechanic and let me assist or do you want to assist me?" I asked.

"I am not sure. How hard is it?"

"It really is easy. Unscrew the inflow and outflow lines, unbolt the pump and replace it. Biggest part is being sure that you plug the inflow line so you don't get gas dripping in your face."

"That I can do, C.J. You assist me."

"Sounds like a plan to me. I'll block the wheels so she won't roll, and you get the toolbox out of the garage. And be sure to put on the overalls hanging up by the door."

Travis crawled under the car while I showed him where the pump was. I handed him the 5/8-inch, open-end wrench. "Undo the inflow line first. Use this to plug the end," I said, as I handed him the rubber stopper.

"Which one is the inflow?"

"Should be the line coming in from the rear where the fuel tank is."

"Well, duh. That makes sense." A few moments passed, and then Travis said, "Okay, inflow and outflow are off. What size wrench fits the pump bolts?"

"Try the 5/8th in your hand and tell me if we need smaller or larger."

"Well, it doesn't fit . . . too big."

Then I handed him a 1/2-inch wrench. "Just right," Travis said.

"Okay, now use the open-end wrench on one side and this socket wrench on the other."

Fifteen minutes later the new pump was installed. A smile spread across the corners of Travis's mouth as he rolled out from under the car. I tossed him the keys and told him to crank her as I got into the passenger seat. "It's your handiwork, so you get to check it out."

The old girl roared to life. "Good job, Travis. Now, let 'er rip."

Travis smiled, "Where to?"

"Not off the property, but thanks to your mom and her horses, you have plenty of trails to ride on. Just take it easy."

"What do you think?" I inquired later as Travis parked the car on the drive outside the kitchen door.

"I think it's ready for the Fall Motorama, weekend after next, except for that weird sound in the old girl's front area."

"We'll call the Tappet Brother's Saturday morn and get their opinion."

"Are you serious?" Travis grinned his mother's wide-open grin as we both got out of the car.

"Sure am. Other than that weird noise, she's perfect inside and out. Our work has paid off." We both stood quietly and admired our months of detailing the old Volvo. We had even taken off the chrome to polish it and then replaced it. The upholstery of dark burgundy was in unusually good shape, especially with everything I had thrown in the back seat during my college years. The gray paint still shown after we waxed it.

"Go on in and finish your homework. I'm going to check on your mother."

The sun had gone down behind the trees, leaving a soft dusk. The riding ring lights had already auto-matically turned on. I walked over to where Hannah sat. She was in her usual place outside the ring with her loyal unfaltering attention on Leeta and Ajax. I also became fixated on this striking woman and her regal horse as they moved around the ring. Ajax moved with effortless grace as he turned on his haunches, trotted forward, then leg yielded sideward, halted, turned on his forehand, canter departed forward and pranced in place. Who would ever believe the agility and grace of an animal weighing half a ton or more? Leeta held her reins with soft hands; her legs hung long and quiet along Ajax's sides as she sat in an upright position. Only her seat moved in perfect rhythm with Ajax's movements. Leeta and Ajax were as one, separate and together and in perfect harmony. Something Leeta and I were not.

Chapter Six
Uncensored, Plainspoken Kate

"GOOD MORNING, C.J.," KATE SAID, AS I WALKED PAST HER open office door.

"Oh, good morning, Kate." I stopped abruptly just past the door and walked backward a few steps, putting me squarely in front of her open door. Pictures of her children and grandchildren covered her walls, and two beautiful orchids sat on her windowsill. Right outside her window, she had placed two bird feeders, and currently there were two blue finches feeding from them.

Kate stopped typing and looked up at me. "What are you looking at C.J.?"

"The finches right outside your window."

Kate turned around to look out the window too. "Oh, yes," she laughed. "I love those little birds. Did you know they're blue in the winter and turn yellow in the spring?"

"No."

She turned back around and faced me. She placed her right arm on her desk, drew up her other arm and rested her chin on the palm of her hand. "They certainly do. I love watching birds. You can learn so much from them. Once they choose their mates, they are lovers for life. They fight. They make up. They have families. They work together to care for each other and their young. They teach their young how to take care of themselves. They don't hold on to them. They shoo them out of the nest when it's time. They mourn. They pick themselves up and begin again."

"Oh," was all I said. Kate had a way of giving double messages with her stories. I knew one was simple, one of her *National Geographic* Specials on wildlife, and this one was about birds. The other was for me. All I could think to say to get relief from this awkward moment was to divert, "Did you get the message from Robert regarding the New York project?"

"Yeah, regarding more insulation needed than what we projected." Kate did what I expected. I knew she wouldn't push me into talking, but I knew she would be there if or when I needed to. "David has already shipped the insulation. It should be there by tomorrow."

I asked, "Robert's out till tomorrow with the job in Tennessee?"

"Yes," Kate responded.

"Okay." I walked into my office and sat at my desk. I looked at my drawings of the new plastic-forming machine. I had hopes it would better streamline how we made the PVC jackets for the insulation. I turned around and looked at the pictures of Leeta and Travis smiling at me. I couldn't stay focused. Yesterday's session was another emotional wipe-out for me. Cullen's complaints kept haunting me, but this time, Leeta was saying them. Chills ran down my spine and turned into a hot sweat. Jane Levy's words that couples marry for the right reasons, but fail because they didn't work out the balance needed, were on a constant rewind-play-again CD in my brain. As an engineer, I readily appreciated the importance of balance needed for any machine to run smoothly. Why was I so amiss in understanding this in my relationship with Leeta? Better yet, how is it that a horse can figure out how to be in perfect harmony with Leeta and I can't?

"C.J.," Kate said, as she walked into my office.

I spun around. I could only stare at her.

"I'm going to deposit these checks at the bank and pick up supplies at Sinclair Office Supply downtown," Kate said hesitantly. "I'm running out of almost everything, especially computer paper and ink. Do you need anything?"

Do I need anything? I thought. *I'm sure I do. I always need something.* I looked at my drawings on the drafting board.

"C.J., what's wrong with you?" Kate clipped. "For the past few weeks you've been real distracted."

"Distracted, that noticeable?" Why was I surprised? Kate has known me for more than fifteen years.

"That noticeable," Kate replied. "Well . . .?"

"Leeta and I are going to a marriage counselor. Yesterday was our second session."

"Uh huh."

"You're not surprised?"

"Surprised wasn't what I was thinking." Kate paused. "It's about time."

"About time?"

"Yes, about time. You picked the best person for you the first time. And you didn't pick the wrong person the second time either."

"What?" I was astonished.

"You married Cullen because you loved her, right?"

"Yes."

"And Leeta?

"Yes."

"Like I said, about time."

"Well, what's yours and Marvin's magic in staying not just married, but happily married?"

"No magic, just a lot of hard work. Like the success of this business—no magic, just a lot of hard work, but work you love to do," she said, as she turned around and headed for the open door.

That's the other thing about Kate, she never minces words. Her steely uncensored plainspokenness sometimes laid me flat, like now.

I again spun my desk chair around to look at the smiling pictures of Leeta, Travis and me. As I did, I saw from the large window on my back wall, a gray fox run along the woods' edge before darting back into them. I smiled, knowing he would be safe, at least from any foxhunt. The cycle of life was always on display just outside my office window. It had been a crimson fall. The woods had been aflame with fall color. The trees were now losing their foliage. In the distance, I could see the Blue Ridge Mountains topped with purple blue hue. I loved this time of year. I felt the tension ease that I had built up since yesterday's session. Our homework assignment was again the same, to have fun and not talk about any of the issues.

"C.J."

I rotated back around. David was standing in front of my desk.

"It's ten-thirty. Are we still on for today?" David asked.

"Huh?"

"You know, we're to go over some stats on the Tennessee project. Also to take a look see at your drawings on the new plastic-forming machine."

"Oh, that's right. I'm not where I had hoped with drafting the update. And Robert is held up in Tennessee for another day, so we really can't do much without his input."

"Hmm, okay. So, lunch then?"

"Well, I don't know. Leeta's to call if she can get away from the farm for lunch."

"Okay."

"Tomorrow at ten-thirty, we'll meet when Robert is back at the plant."

"Tomorrow then," David said, as he began to walk out the door.

"David."

"Yeah?"

"You and Sarah have been married now for fifteen good years?"

"Yep, fifteen years, about the time I started working here at the plant."

"And your sons?"

"All growing as fast as weeds. Michael will be ten in December. And Sam, eight, is almost as tall as Michael. Josh can hold his own and him being only five."

"You and Sarah?"

"She and the kids keep me hopping, but I wouldn't want it any other way."

"What's your magic?"

"Magic?" David paused. "I don't understand."

"To a happy marriage."

"Look what we've accomplished here at International Commercial Insulations through commitment and loving the work we do. As Kate has always said about the success of this business, 'No magic, C.J., commitment and hard work, but work you love to do.' That's what makes the success in anything you do, be it your marriage, your kids, or work. No magic, C.J., none at all," David said, as he walked out of my office.

Well the consensus is in, I thought. *No magic remedy, just hard work, but work you love to do.*

Chapter Seven

Living Issues

"Hello," Jane said, greeting us in the waiting room and directing us to the room where the last two sessions had been held. "How was your week?"

We both waited for the other to begin. I sat quietly mulling over my having several sleepless nights and my dreams being blurred as to who were in the dreams, Leeta or Cullen. But what did remain consistent in every dream was the arguing between Leeta or Cullen and me. Their arguing with me drove either one to tears, and my burying myself into whatever I was doing at the time to avoid them. All I knew was I felt comfortable and safe doing anything else other than arguing. When I woke, I could never remember what the argument was about, but just what I was doing—working on the Volvo, drafting ideas for another machine, making contacts on the ham radio.

"Well?" Jane asked looking directly at me.

"Well, the week was pleasant," I replied cautiously paranoid. "Leeta's great home-cooked meals . . . but that's standard fare. We had a nice family weekend with Travis. Friday night, we went to the high school football game and then to the homecoming dance to hear Travis play his saxophone with the high school jazz band. As a family, we had fun on a trail ride at DuPont Forest on Sunday. Travis and I did stuff together too. We worked on the Volvo Tuesday evening. Saturday morning, we called the Tappet Brothers on *NPR's Car Talk* regarding some weird sound we had heard in the right front tire area."

"Really? You were able to get through?" Jane asked.

"Yep, sure did."

Jane laughed. "Definitely a memory maker."

"Yeah. Travis couldn't believe I picked up the phone to call them. We really loved their banter about the Volvo, and how we were sprucing her up."

"Were they able to help?"

"Yep. We all agreed it didn't sound like a big deal. The Tappet Brothers thought it was a small rock caught in the wheel well or hub cab of the right tire. It was the wheel well." I looked over at Leeta who sat motionless and expressionless. To avoid any possibility of an argument between us, I decided not to add that Travis asked if he could date in the Volvo when he got his license and that the car had become as magical and dear to him as to me. "No fighting, but then again, we weren't to talk about the issues." *Did I get it right this time? Just because we had fun and enjoyed each other, doesn't mean we're fine. Leeta's big point from last session.*

Jane looked at Leeta, "And you?"

"The same, pleasant enough. But, I feel C.J. has been distracted most of the week. I'm convinced he's always at work in his head, even though he says he's not. This distraction of his leaves me feeling I have to walk a tightrope."

Jane turned to me. "Do you agree with Leeta's assumption?"

"I've heard this before from Leeta. I've tried hard to leave work at work, but Leeta doesn't believe me. But, yes, this week I've been distracted, but not about work, about us."

"So Leeta is *partially* correct."

"Yes. My distraction was about what was said last session about people marrying the right person, and their marriage ending in divorce because they didn't find the balance needed to live together happily. And Leeta's complaints aren't unlike Cullen's complaints. It's daunting. I guess I'm feeling a little pinched."

"Scared?" Jane was now looking directly into my eyes. It was the second time I've been asked that this month. I prided myself in the tough man image. It had been a necessity for me. As a child, I knew of no other choice. Between the blows of my stepfather, the self-absorption of my mother, and my father consumed with making a living, there was nobody watching over me. I had to develop my tough man's armor.

I reluctantly echoed Jane's question, "Scared? Yes, because I know Leeta is the right person for me, and I don't want to lose her or her son, Travis. And if our marriage fails, I will lose both of them." *There, I finally admitted I'm afraid.*

"C.J. is there more?" Jane asked quietly.

I really didn't want to, but respecting Jane's statement in our first session of her being as good as the information given her, I pushed myself to say more. "Yes, there's more. With my last marriage, I thought I was doing all the right things. I thought Cullen's complaints were silly, and she was just being selfish. But now that I'm hearing the same complaints, it has me thinking that it's me with the problems." I looked at Leeta who was sitting with her back facing me. The anxiety I was feeling was indescribable, and Leeta's silence made it even more profound inside my wrenching gut. *This is the hardest thing I've ever done, admitting to myself I have a problem and then telling somebody else, who just happens to be my wife.*

Thankfully, Jane disrupted the deafening quiet that had penetrated the room with her pronouncement, "It takes two to be in a relationship, meaning Cullen and you both participated in its failures as well as its successes. It's not just you. The same is true for Leeta and you. In the first session, I said you're a normal couple dealing with normal issues, which are inherent in any relationship to some degree. Do you remember what I called them?"

I just remembered we were a normal couple, but that was all.

"Living issues." Jane stopped and looked at both of us. "I said the easy part in a relationship is falling in love, and that the hard part is negotiating the balance needed for two people to live together. The need for this balance is more intense when children, animals or just life circumstances are added. And this balance becomes more difficult to achieve, because there are more tradeoffs to negotiate when these additions are made."

"Tradeoffs?" I asked.

"Yes, tradeoffs—the sharing a bed or a closet with your bride, which family or friend you visit or not visit during the holidays, your once uninterrupted sleep being replaced by the three a.m. feeding of your newborn, or your partner snoring." The afternoon sun streamed through the window, illuminating Jane's eyes, so they were even greener than usual. There was definitely a no-nonsense approach about her. She meant for us to work with her. "You've named two already. Both of you talked about the home maintenance issue. C.J., you felt Leeta to be too picky. Leeta, you describe C.J. as not involved enough in the care of the home. You, Leeta, talked about your being off balance in your time apart and time together living issue, Correct?"

We both nodded. *Jeez, this woman doesn't forget a thing,* I thought. *How does she remember everything we tell her, much less everything else she hears?*

"There can be extended family issues, but I didn't hear any from you two. I understood Leeta to say that

C.J., you joined her on special occasions with her family. C.J., I didn't hear you express any concerns about your family or Leeta's. Are there?"

"Well." I paused, remembering vividly that Cullen and my mother didn't get along and my refusing to discuss my mother with Cullen.

"C.J., are there any extended family issues with your family or with Leeta's?"

"No."

"Leeta, with C.J.'s family?"

"I didn't meet C.J.'s father. He died before we met. His mother, I've never met actually. She lives in Houston with her second husband. There's an older sister too. She moves quite a bit due to her job. She calls every now and then. There's just not much contact with his family."

Jane looked in my direction. I looked back. I didn't want to discuss my family with Jane either. Working on my marriage was enough. That was all I could do now.

"Generally, work on extended family issues," Jane continued, "centers on boundaries being clearly defined and agreed upon."

"Boundaries?" Leeta queried.

"Yes, boundaries. It's not necessary that the in-laws, siblings and grown children are liked, even though that is what is usually preferred. However, respect for each other is a must. The primary issues are when extended families are to visit, for how long, and how involved they can be in your life together. And the couple clearly defining and maintaining these boundaries with their extended families. It seems with your father being dead, your mother being so far away and a sister whose main contact is an occasional phone call, your extended family boundaries were already built in before you met Leeta."

"Yes, you could say that," I responded. *And thankfully,* I thought.

Jane continued, "Money, I didn't hear any, except for Leeta being relieved bills were paid and nothing held back. Are there any?"

"Well, Leeta has her money, which she earns from her work with the horses and her child support. It's hers to do as she likes. I pay most of the big bills such as the mortgage, insurances, utilities and the like. I think we're good with the money."

"Leeta?" asked Jane.

I noted Leeta didn't answer right away. In fact, her neck began to grow bright red patches that multiplied rapidly as they covered her entire neck and marched up her face.

"What? Is there more stuff that doesn't satisfy you about me?" I asked hesitantly.

Leeta took a deep breath and said, "I guess I do have issues about the money, but I never felt I had a right to complain, because it is C.J.'s money and not mine."

"What are you talking about, Leeta?" I could feel the heat rise up from my chest and my armpits get sticky again from my sweat.

"You're stingy."

"Stingy? Stingy?" I repeated again in disbelief. "I bought you a horse farm and a beautiful Victorian home with a wraparound porch."

"Yes, you did, but the house required and still requires a lot of renovations that you pay for because I can't. And I don't hear the end of it! How expensive it was to replace the rotten siding or the new roof, or to rewire the house! The list goes on and on."

"God!" I interrupted, as I threw up my hands in exasperation.

"C.J., breathe," Jane said calmly.

"Breathe. Hell, I'm not going to breathe. Apparently, I don't satisfy this woman! She's a bottomless pit."

"Listen!" Jane stated forcefully. She looked at each of us independently. I didn't open my mouth nor did

Leeta. "It's obvious that your and Leeta's way isn't working," Jane stated emphatically, "and just how do I know that? It's because I'm sure you wouldn't be wasting your time or your money with me, if your way was working."

"Yes," I responded slowly. I was taken aback with her sternness. It was so incongruent with her diminutive stature.

"Okay, folks, we need to breathe. Get yourself comfortable and close your eyes." In an instant, Jane's tone changed from forceful to soothing.

I looked over at Leeta. Her face was as red as one of those fireball candies, which burn like hell after the first few seconds of sucking on them. Damn, I was pissed. *You can't tell me I haven't made life better for you, I thought. When is enough going to be enough for you? You would still be leasing five acres from old man Collins with that scraggily-ass wire fence bordering it, and that decrepit shed that was dangerous for anyone to be in, much less the horses.*

"C.J., close your eyes," Jane demanded.

"All right," I responded in a huff.

"Leeta, you too. Thank you. Okay then, follow my directives. Take a deep breath, notice what your body feels like each time your chest falls, notice your body becoming quieter and quieter," Jane stated in a soothing tone, but she stopped abruptly. "C.J., slow it down. You're going to hyperventilate and pass out."

Not a bad idea, I thought.

"C.J., follow my directives. You both said you wanted to stop the loud mean arguments with no resolutions. This is the first step, to become calm. Close your eyes again," Jane demanded.

I closed my eyes reluctantly.

"Thank you. All right, close your eyes, get comfortable and take an easy breath in, noticing what your body feels like each time your chest falls." Jane talked in the same slow, calm rhythm as in the last session. "That's good, Leeta. A little slower, C.J."

I nodded. I could feel myself become calmer.

"Again, take an easy deep breath . . ."

Time stood still. The energy around me seem to soften, a peaceful quiet encircled me. I could hear Jane's voice in the distant background. I could feel my heartbeat and breathing slow down. My head felt light, my fingers were warm and tingly and my legs were heavy, as if they were made of lead.

"Before you open your eyes, allow yourself to become aware of your surroundings by feeling the chair you are sitting in and where your hands are resting. Allow the noises that surround you to come back into your conscious awareness. Now, open your eyes slowly."

"Wow," I said.

"Yes?" Jane asked.

"I feel," I stopped. I was trying to think of the right word to describe my feeling, a feeling I never remember ever having. "I feel peaceful. Yes, peaceful."

"Very good, C.J., and you, Leeta?"

Leeta nodded. The red had gone from her face. The patches on her neck were still there but much fainter.

"Now we're ready to resume. So, there is a money issue. Leeta, you feel C.J. is stingy, and C.J., you feel you are beyond generous with your money, correct?"

"Well, yes," I responded.

"Yes." Leeta responded.

"I'm also hearing there's his/her money, but no *our* money," Jane continued.

"Well, yes," Leeta responded, furrowing her brows, as she often did when mulling things over. "I've never thought of it that way, but we have no *our* money."

"Is that what puts you off balance with the money issue, no *our* money?" Jane asked.

"Yes, I guess so," Leeta said hesitantly. "No. I don't know." Leeta's red neck patches started to darken and multiply again as they began their slow march up her face.

"Hmm," Jane said.

Well, she's right, I thought. *There's no our money. That's simple fact. Damn, has she ever felt deprived being married to me? What does she want from me, a limitless money coffer?* I could feel the heat rise up from my chest again and my shirt sticking to my damp back. I thought, *Take an easy breath in and let go, and again* . . . Jane did not look at me nor did she ask for my opinion. I chose just to stay silent on this one.

"Parenting issues," Jane resumed. "Are there any? This isn't unusual, especially when couples remarry with family."

Leeta looking in my direction said, "Not really. My first husband and I divorced when Travis was barely one. And honestly, after my marriage with Chad, I just didn't want to get married again. I didn't date much either. I was too busy raising Travis and making ends meet. Travis was eight when I met C.J., and we dated several months before I allowed Travis and C.J. to meet. I don't know. Their relationship has evolved on their own terms. I like what I see and continue to see." Leeta paused and as she did, she pressed her lips together and furrowed her brows again. "C.J. is a very honest and straightforward man." She spoke carefully. "I like that about him. He's not pushy. I've appreciated that from the beginning of our relationship. And C.J. told Travis he didn't fall in love with *him*, that he fell in love with *me*. But he promised Travis he would always be fair and good to him. I thought fair enough, and I think it took the pressure off Travis that he had to love this man because I did. I can safely say they fell in love with each other on their own terms, and in their own time. I do know that C.J. thinks of Travis like his own son."

"Do you agree?" Jane asked me.

I responded, "Yes, I do agree. I love that boy, and he knows it." I became quiet with the memories of my yesteryears. *I wanted to offer Travis what wasn't offered to me when my mother remarried, that my stepdad be fair and good to me. That never happened. By the time I was fourteen, my relationship with my stepdad was beyond snide remarks. It had gotten physical. By my fifteenth birthday, I had moved in with my dad and his wife full time and visited my mom on an occasional weekend.*

"I'm impressed," Jane said, interrupting my thoughts.

"Why?" I asked.

"With how you two included Travis in your life together—C.J., your promise to be fair and good to him, and Leeta, your allowing their relationship to evolve on their own terms. That's two gems I need to put in my treasure chest to share with other couples who remarry with family."

"Gems to put in your treasure chest?" I asked.

"Yes, my clients give me gems all the time in how they worked through difficult issues. It's one thing to get married or remarried, but to be remarried with family is another situation altogether. Children don't necessarily blend into their parents' new marriages or families, like we all wish for when we remarry with children. There is no Brady Bunch family outside of TV Land.

It seems the two of you gave Travis two priceless gems for him to figure out how he wanted to be included in your life together. C.J., you promised him you would always be fair and good to him, and Leeta, you got out of their way while they figured it out."

"Hmm," I responded.

Jane resumed, "So, there are no parenting issues creating conflict between the two of you?"

"What do you mean?" I asked.

"Privileges like friend time, curfew, money spent on him. Responsibilities, such as chores around the house or schoolwork. Respect issues, especially as it relates to you being the stepfather. Frequently, stepparents feel they have a lot of responsibility in the care of their stepkids, but little, if any authority with the child, especially in decision making or discipline."

"Well, not really," I said. "Like Leeta said, I met her when Travis was eight. Leeta is a good mother. I'm not his parent and never pretended to be. Travis is a good kid, respectful, easy to be with."

"Not his parent and never pretended to be. You are his stepparent?" Jane queried.

"Well, yes. Let me say it this way. By the time I met Leeta, the ground rules were already set on how he was being raised. Plus, Leeta was very protective of Travis like the lioness with her cub. Yes, I'm his stepparent but not his parent. I don't know. Maybe, I was that stepkid once. I know I resented like hell my stepfather changing the rules. But Travis is a child I can be around. I guess if he wasn't, I would've left the relationship."

"So Leeta's parental values and style you agree with?"

"Well, yes, you could say that. I just knew I couldn't change them, but then again I didn't want to. They made sense to me."

"You agree with what C.J. is saying, Leeta?"

"Yes, he is right. I'm a lioness with her cub. My claws do go out if I think Travis is in any kind of harm's way. My rules are set. And like I've already said, I like what I see and continue to see between C.J. and Travis. My only complaint is more of his time—not just for me, but also for Travis."

"Yes, the time together, time apart issue. The other relationship issue that Leeta brought up was sex. If I remember correctly, Leeta, you're saying you were having many of the same fights you had with your first husband and one of the fighting issues being around sex. Correct?"

"Yes." Leeta nodded. "I don't know. Sometimes I think that sex is the only thing on men's minds."

"It is," Jane said, her eyes smiling.

"Really?" Leeta blurted back.

"Is that correct?" Jane looked at me.

"Well, yes," I responded.

"And the alleged reports say that men think about sex on the average every seven seconds. You agree, C.J.?"

"Well, maybe not every *seven* seconds."

Leeta broke in, her mouth dropping open, "Oh gosh, so I'm married . . ."

"To a man—a very healthy, normal man at that," Jane inserted.

*　*　*

"Well, it's good to know we're normal," I said guardedly to Leeta on our drive home.

"Yeah," Leeta said, looking at me out the corner of her eye. "So every seven seconds men think about sex. I'm exhausted just thinking about it. Do you guys think about anything else?"

I laughed nervously.

"What's so funny?" Leeta quipped.

"I don't know, maybe your astonishment."

"Well, I *am* astonished. Is it true?"

"Every seven seconds sounds a little much, but I do think most men think about sex a lot." I paused, glancing in her direction. She had her hair pulled up as I liked, and soft wisps of her hair had fallen as usual, framing her face. Her brows were furrowed again, but after today's session, I didn't find this expression as appealing as I had in the past. One thing for sure, I did understand from our sessions, we were not ready to discuss anything without Ms. Levy's help. "Remember now, our homework assignment is still not to talk about the issues, but to have fun," I stressed.

"Sure," Leeta said insipidly. "And for us each to bring to the next session an issue we want to work on."

"Yeah, that's right," I said, turning into our driveway.

"I bet I can guess what you want to do for fun," Leeta said coolly, turning toward me.

Her dark brown eyes, lined with her long rich eyelashes, looked straight into my eyes, sending chills down my spine. *Certainly not this week,* I thought.

"Ajax had a mild colic this morning. I'm going to check on him. You and Travis eat without me," Leeta said, opening her car door once the Volvo was parked. Hannah, as always, waited on Leeta, and together they walked toward the barn.

Travis opened the kitchen door, stepped aside and looked expectantly at me.

"Your mom said for us eat without her," I said as I came in. My nostrils quickly filled up with the pleasant smell of baked apple. I straightaway spied atop the wood stove the apple crisp alongside a baked spaghetti casserole, two of my favorite dishes.

"What's up with Mom?" Before I could answer, Travis added, "She's upset, isn't she?"

I don't know. She might be, I thought. I opted simply to ask a question, "Why do you ask?"

"Mom doesn't miss the family meal unless she's really upset."

I felt foolish. He was right. "Well, she said Ajax had a mild colic this morning, and she wanted to check on him." It was all I could say.

"Yeah, she told me she gave him a shot of Banamine, and he worked himself out of it in less than thirty minutes. She told me he was okay. I've checked on him a couple of times, and he's still fine. I would have called her on her cell if he wasn't."

"Oh. Well, let me see what's going on then," I said feigning confidence. I walked outside and headed toward the barn. I stopped like I was immersed in cement. I saw Leeta sitting bareback on Ajax in the barnyard. She had leaned forward, resting her head on his muscled neck, and her arms hung limp over his withers. Hannah sat quietly at the barn door with her ears perked up and her unfaltering devotion directed toward Leeta.

Once again, I found myself envious of the relationship between Ajax and Leeta. I wanted more than anything to take her in my arms and hold her close to me, to brush my lips against her silken hair and to smell the slight scent of lavender, which always perfumed her body. If she only knew the power she had over me. One touch and I'm hers. I would be right there waiting for her next command on bended knee. Ajax looked over at me, as if he knew of my longing, and neighed softly as he walked away, taking his lady with him.

Chapter Eight

Outdoorsman Robert

I SMELLED THE COFFEE AS SOON AS I WALKED INTO THE PLANT'S back door. "Good morning, Kate," I said, sticking my head into her office's door. Doughnuts too, I duly noted as I passed the table where the coffeepot and mugs sat in the waiting area. "What's the occasion . . . birthday, anniversary?"

"No occasion, just a little something to knock the November chill off . . . in and out of the office," Kate said calmly as she closed the top filing cabinet drawer. "I got away from the house early this morning and went by McFarlan. The doughnuts were fresh from the fryer."

"Hmmm," I said as I poured myself a cup of coffee and spied the chocolate covered cake doughnuts. They were my absolute favorite because of the rich chocolate coating. I wondered, *If it could be that simple, fresh doughnuts could knock the chill off at home and resolve our marriage woes too.* I looked out the large, oak-trimmed windows that framed the waiting area. Many of the trees had lost their leaves, and the leaves that were left on the branches were brown. As I took my first sip of coffee and was about to sink my teeth into one of the chocolate doughnuts, two gray foxes ran together along our grassy courtyard and scurried across the gravel drive into the woods.

"Wow, aren't they beautiful?" Kate whispered. "You know, I've never seen a fox here before. I've always seen deer running across the plant's yard into the woods, and even more the last few years."

"Yes, I've noticed more too. Robert said he saw a bear at his place a few weekends ago," I said with a sigh. Developers from all over were coming to Hendersonville and buying up mountainsides, farmland and apple orchards. "Kate, when you see Robert, tell him I'm in my office. I need an update on the Tennessee and New York projects."

"Sure," she replied, carefully placing a postage stamp on a letter.

I knew she wanted to talk more. She and her family had lived in Hendersonville for generations. I had no magic answer as how to preserve the beauty and uniqueness of Hendersonville. I had hopes I could make a difference being on the city planning board. Our city leaders were more and more voting down our recommendations for preservation and voting on the side of the developer. As one angry shop owner said, "These developers aren't helping us as they claim. All they're doing is capitalizing on our success."

At the first city council meeting of our newly elected mayor, a Florida developer presented his plans for an eighty-foot high-rise condo, which was against the city's sixty-four-foot height ordinance. City residents protested every way they could. City Hall was flooded with letters, phone calls and e-mails. People demonstrated with their signs. We didn't want our downtown buildings to be any taller than sixty-four feet. We didn't want to be a Charlotte or even an Asheville. This didn't matter to our elected officials. One city council member justified his support for downtown condo high-rises saying, "It would mitigate the sprawl in the county. Better to go up than out." This became his mantra.

The representing attorney for the developer proclaimed loudly, "The bigger, the better."

Another council member announced boldly, "Build those suckers and build them on every corner."

The Mayor, joining the other two council members in the yes vote for downtown high-rises, insisted the people elected him to represent the people by doing what he knew was best for the people. In a three-to-two vote, the eighty-foot height amendment won approval, giving the go ahead to the eighty-foot high-rise condo.

I, along with the rest of the planning board members and city residents, was astounded. We felt betrayed and more so by our newly elected mayor. He was the hometown boy, whose campaign platform was to protect and preserve Hendersonville for our children and grandchildren.

Tossing my coat on the couch, I walked to my desk, sat down, popped the last bite of the doughnut into my mouth and took another sip of coffee to wash it down. I glanced over at the final draft of the new pipefitting machine. I was not pleased. Both David and Robert were noncommittal in giving me their opinion. My hope was the new machine would streamline the production of the PVC pipefittings. I had been excited about building this one, especially since the sales of the fittings were quickly becoming the largest part of the plant's business. With the increasing tensions at home, I found myself being distracted with my thoughts of Leeta and her stated dissatisfactions with me in counseling. Was counseling really working? Sometimes I felt it was only making matters worse. I dreaded next week's session, as well as going home to Leeta. The disdain from her last night was unnerving. We barely talked, and she positioned herself so far on the other side of the bed, she might as well have been in the other room.

I heard a tap, tap on the window behind me. As I turned around, I saw Robert smiling, beckoning me to come outside as he bit into a doughnut he was holding. He had a cup of coffee in the other hand.

"No, too chilly," I mouthed.

Again, he smiled with a wave of his hand to come out.

"Why not," I thought as I retrieved my coat, refilled my coffee and grabbed one more doughnut from the table in the waiting area.

"It just feels too good out here to be stuck inside. Come on. Let's take a walk through the woods," Robert said as I walked toward him.

As the deer and foxes had done, we walked along the woods' edge before escaping into the safety and serenity of the trees. We walked slowly along, enjoying the quiet. A thick bed of leaves covered most of the woods' floor, and the morning sun peeked through the trees, presenting patches of her gold along the way. We broke off the well-worn path and meandered along to each other's whims.

Yumm, I thought as I finished the doughnut and took the last swallow of my coffee. *A cup of coffee never tasted better than with something sweet. It was the perfect match.*

"Well," Robert said. "Everything is going according to plan with both projects. No complaints from anyone."

"Great. I plan to begin work on the new machine."

"If you need anyone to assist you, I'm your guy."

"Great."

"So when do we start?"

"Actually, this project should have been well on its way. I'm just not pleased with my design yet."

"Been distracted?"

"Well, yeah."

"Leeta?"

"Yeah," I said. *Jeez,* I thought, *am I so obvious with my feelings? Leeta, Kate and now Robert?*

"And."

"We're seeing a marriage counselor, Jane Levy. Yesterday was our third session."

"And."

"We're discovering we're a normal couple," I lied. I didn't tell him I didn't feel normal, and that I was scared my marriage would be in the half that failed.

"What do you mean?"

"Every couple deals with the same struggles, once they start living together. The challenge is to work out this stuff, so they can live together happily, and . . . in harmony," I said quietly. *Something Ajax had figured out quite successfully with Leeta,* I reflected. *Damn horse.*

"What stuff?"

"Money, upkeep of the home, children, relatives, how you spend your time together, sex. Jane Levy calls these living issues."

"Interesting . . . I thought I just married the same woman twice. I had the same arguments with Alice that I had with Rachael. They just looked different and had different names. I just figured I made poor choices with the women I fell in love with."

"Jane Levy says that divorce isn't due to your marrying the wrong person. It's because the couple didn't negotiate the balance needed with their living issues."

"Balance?"

"Yes, balance, like the balance needed with my machine parts for the machine to run smoothly."

"Maybe I should have gone to marriage counseling with Alice. She had asked, in fact *pleaded* with me. Too late now, I've been through two divorces. That's enough for me. I'm a confirmed bachelor," Robert avowed, digging his hands into his jeans pockets. His boyish grin evaporated and his shoulders slumped as he turned away and walked ahead. I stood still and watched him disappear around the bend.

Robert's heart was broken with his divorce from Alice. I remembered how drawn and tired he looked. I saw that same look in me now. "Do I just make poor choices with women?" he had asked me after they separated. "This just doesn't make sense to me. I married Alice because I loved her and enjoyed her company. We had so much in common. We didn't rush the relationship. We took time in getting to know each other. I thought she was perfect for me. What happened?"

At the time, I didn't know what to say to Robert. Now I did. *The hard part of the relationship isn't the loving but the living. The solution is finding the balance. I should know how to do that. I'm an engineer.*

Chapter Nine

Loud, Mean Arguments

"**H**OW WAS YOUR WEEK?" JANE ASKED US AS WE SAT IN THE counseling room chairs.

I wasn't going to begin this session. As far as I was concerned, the week had gone from bad to worse. We'd barely spoken to each other, much less looked at each other.

"Well," Leeta said, "we had no arguments."

"Ah, you had no arguments. Did you have fun together?"

"It's been quiet," Leeta replied.

"Quiet. Huh. C.J., how was the week for you?"

"Like Leeta said, quiet, no arguments." I was following Leeta's lead. At this point, I felt no matter what I did or said it was going to be wrong.

"My question still hasn't been answered."

Leeta said nothing. She just crossed her arms in front of her chest and abruptly shifted her position away from me. Instead of looking at Jane or me, she faced the wall that had all of Jane's diplomas and professional licenses. Damn it, pissed didn't even come close to the anger I felt. "No, we didn't have fun," I said flatly.

"Why?" Jane asked quietly.

"He didn't even ask to have fun," Leeta sneered. "He just hibernated in his study in the evenings, playing on that damn ham radio, and the entire weekend he worked with Robert on his new machine."

"Quite frankly, I didn't think Leeta wanted to do anything fun, and I wasn't going to push it." I restrained myself from saying, *Stop hugging that damn horse of yours; then I'll stop hugging my damn ham radio. As far as Robert, you didn't make any offers. He did.*

"Stop," Jane stated emphatically. "What changed from the week before that you two stopped enjoying each other?"

"Why bother?" Leeta snipped. "Yes, we've had good weeks together, and then we get in here and C.J. just explodes. How many times have you told C.J. to breathe, so he'll calm down so we can just get through the session?"

"Your point?" Jane asked.

"What *is* the point is more like it?" Leeta scoffed.

"Okay then. Yes, C.J. has expressed anger in session, and so have you, Leeta. And you both came in expressing concerns about your loud, mean arguments with no resolutions. I'm confused about your annoyance with the anger, since it was identified as an issue and a counseling goal by both of you. Again, I ask you, what changed?"

"To me, it appears counseling is not helping. We are blowing up in counseling like we do at home. I don't feel any safer here than I do there," Leeta stated emphatically.

"What do you mean?" Jane asked.

"Well, we have never been physically violent with each other, but I'm afraid it will happen.

"I see C.J. explode a lot quicker in here than he does at home. Counseling isn't working. It just makes matters worse."

"Then what do you want to do?"

"What do *you* mean?"

"Well, Leeta, if marriage counseling isn't working, what do you propose to do about your unhappy marriage?" Jane asked calmly.

"I don't know. That's the problem, I don't know."

"A divorce?" Jane queried.

God, a divorce! I screamed to myself. My heart was pounding so hard and fast I could hear it pulsating in my ears.

"A divorce, what are you talking about? I never said I wanted a divorce." Leeta responded in an agitated tone.

"Then help me out here, Leeta. You decide on counseling because you're unhappy with the marriage. Now you're saying counseling isn't working, and that it only makes matters worse. What do you want to do? What's left?"

Leeta looked straight ahead. There were no red patches marching from the nook of her neck, over her jaw and up her cheek. In fact, her face had a grayish pallor, her lips were drawn thin, and her eyes were dark pools of emptiness. "No, I don't want a divorce," Leeta said slowly as she turned her emptiness toward me. "I don't feel safe saying anything in counseling because I'm afraid you'll start yelling. I'm sorry I can't shut off what happens here and go home with you to have fun. That's a dumb assignment anyway."

Talking about fear, I thought, *it's growing wildly inside of me. What do I say? Everything she is saying is true. The anger I was feeling at the beginning of the session has now dissipated into a puddle of unadulterated fear. I'm soaking in it. My shirt from my armpits down to the center of my rib cage is saturated. I can feel my entire hairline from my forehead to the base of my neck, sopping wet with perspiration. One would think I have just run a marathon with my street clothes on, and I have, except it is an emotional marathon.*

"C.J., what's happening?" Jane asked.

"I don't know what's happening," I responded back.

"Let me ask it another way. Are you okay?"

I screamed to myself, *"My God, woman, it doesn't take a genius to realize I'm not okay! I'm sweating bullets here. My heart is pounding out of my chest. I'm sure I'm going to have a heart attack any minute, and my wife looks like something has just sucked out her soul. And that something is apparently me!*

"C.J.," I heard a faint, but familiar voice that seemed to come from miles away.

"C.J.," I heard it again, and a gentle hand touched my arm. I turned toward the voice. It was Leeta. Her eyes had softened now, and the color had returned to her face. Instead of seeing a woman whose features appeared chiseled in stone, I saw a woman whose face was full of worry.

"Leeta, I simply don't know what to say or do," I whispered.

"C.J. and Leeta, I want you to take a few minutes to breathe, to calm down and to get your bodies back to a state of homeostasis, a state of balance." Jane looked carefully at the two of us.

Leeta nodded as did I. I was desperate. I'd do anything. I was sure I was going to either have a stroke or suffocate to death with the emotions that were welling up in the back of my throat.

"Close your eyes and get yourself comfortable," Jane began in the soft monotone voice as before. "Follow my directives to the best of your ability. Breathe in, take an easy deep breath in, and let go, noticing what your body does each time your chest falls . . . good. Again . . . feel your body get calmer and calmer, quieter and . . . ." Jane's voice blurred into a rhythmic easy hum. The sounds from outside of Jane's window and the soothing tick tock of Jane's table clock blended into the beat of her hum. With each exhale, I felt a relaxing relief. My heartbeat slowed its pace. Better, better, I felt. The peaceful energy of last session's breathing exercise surrounded me again. Except this time, I felt it weaved itself in and out every fiber of me.

Then I heard Jane's comforting voice, "Leeta, C.J., before you open your eyes, allow yourself to become aware of your surroundings by feeling the chair you are sitting in, where your hands are resting, and allow the noises that surround you to come back into your conscious awareness."

I felt myself gradually come up deep from within me. As my eyelids pulled themselves open, I was back in my chair. I knew I didn't go anywhere, but that's how I felt, back in my chair. I knew the place I had been was in my mind. I looked at Jane's clock. It was silent now. Odd, each tick tock of the clock had been so well articulated, and only ten minutes had passed. This time I felt I had relaxed much longer. Different from last session, when I felt I had relaxed a shorter period and had not.

"Good. Now, open your eyes," Jane said quietly.

We both sat still. I was perfectly content to stay put until session's end, just to savor the calm I felt so deeply, lest I never experienced it again.

"Well, Leeta," Jane said carefully. "I don't think I ever said counseling was going to be easy. But through the counseling process, the emotions embedded in your issues will eventually be diffused; then you'll be able to be more task oriented. When this occurs, the issues are no longer problems, but challenges you want to conquer. Counseling becomes an adventure of growth, not just for you as individuals, but also for the marriage."

"Leeta, this is just our fourth session," Jane continued. "For the past three sessions, I have asked you and C.J. to educate me. I do understand educating me is hard on the two of you because you're hearing what you don't like about each other, or what you feel the other is doing wrong. This evokes anger, which is actually evoked by chemicals being secreted from your brain. The release of these is the brain's barometer of letting you know how important these issues are to you. But this anger that you are screaming at each other could also be a cover up for your fears."

"Fears?" Leeta responded.

"Yes, fears. The next time you become angry, ask yourself not why am I angry but what am I afraid of? So Leeta, do you want to continue?"

Leeta turned toward me. Her eyes that had been deep, dark abysses of emptiness earlier had softened and converted into deep bowls of rich, dark warm chocolate. I could fall right into them and just melt into oblivion. *How can this woman inspire such passion from me and incite such rage?*

"Yes," Leeta said.

Thank you, I thought, *but I knew her answer before she said it. Her eyes always told on her.*

"C.J.?" Jane asked.

"Yes," I said without hesitation.

"Good. As for the other part of your homework assignment, you both have an issue to present?"

Yes, I thought to myself, *But who wants to be the first to rock the boat?* We both were quiet. I wondered if Leeta felt the same way. I noted we looked at Jane Levy and not at each other.

"Issues. Who wants to begin first?"

"Well." Leeta spoke slowly and looked at me. "I can begin first."

"Good," Jane responded, "but before you start, I have some ground rules. This exercise attends to each of your goals to learn better communication and end the mean, loud fighting that has no resolutions. There is a speaker and a listener. Leeta, since you'll be presenting your issue first, you're the speaker. You may take all the time you need to say everything you want to say. Your only responsibility is for you to make sure C.J.

understands your information *exactly* as you want him to understand it."

"Yes," Leeta responded warily.

"You'll understand better when I explain the ground rules to C.J. And I'll be coaching you two through this speaker-listener exercise."

Jane turned toward me. "And C.J., you're the listener. Your only responsibility is to understand Leeta's information *exactly* as Leeta wants you to understand it. Stephen Covey says it best in his book, *The Habits of Highly Effective People,* 'Seek first to understand before being understood.'"

I closed my eyes as I committed this phrase to memory, "Seek first to understand before being understood." Jane was quiet. She waited for me to make eye contact with her again.

"I'm giving you three stop tools as aids to accomplish this. You may use these tools at any time and as frequently as you choose. I strongly encourage you to use them since you're responsible for receiving Leeta's information *exactly* as she wants you to understand it."

I took a deep breath. I could feel the heat rise through my body as the word exactly penetrated into my brain. I'm to understand Leeta *exactly* as she wants me to understand her. Exactly . . .

"The first stop tool is called information overload. This means tell Leeta to stop talking before you're saturated with more information than you can possibly remember. To assure Leeta that you understand her information, you will repeat her information back to her. Any questions so far?" Jane paused, looking at both of us. "So far so good," Jane continued. "The second stop tool, C.J., is called information clarification. This stop tool is used when either you don't understand what Leeta is saying, or you don't hear what she's saying, because you're distracted by your own thoughts. Am I clear so far?"

I nodded. It was becoming quite clear that I was to listen to Leeta like I've never listened to her, or for that matter, anyone before.

"Okay, then. Your third stop tool is called lousy approach. Now we all know the obvious lousy approaches. They were your presenting complaints in our first session together—loud arguments, saying hurtful things to each other. Those are definitely lousy approaches. Others are throwing things, breaking things, pushing, shoving, hitting. They weren't identified as approaches either of you have used toward each other, correct?"

We looked at each other.

"Correct?" Jane asked again.

"Well," Leeta said slowly. "We never broke or threw things or were physical with each other. But as I've already said, if we did continue the way we were going, it could have developed into that."

"Hmm," Jane responded softly. "Well, we've already begun working with the anger concerns through the breathing. Today's goal is to seek to understand before being understood, the first step toward your goal to communicate better. Ready, Leeta?"

"Yes," Leeta said as she sat herself even more erect and grasped the arms of the chair.

"One more thing," Jane interrupted, "Leeta, you're to face C.J., not me, because that's who you want to have understand you."

"Oh, yes," Leeta whispered, turning toward me. "Okay then. What I want to present isn't necessarily an issue per se, as much as how I feel when I talk to you." Leeta stopped. Her face flushed and her lips trembled.

"Are you okay?" Jane asked.

"Not exactly. I'm afraid C.J. will be upset with what I'm going to say."

"I assume this concern is some of the cause of the continuous fights."

"Well, yes, it is."

"Then it needs to be presented so you can move forward in working on the challenges in your relationship."

"All right then," Leeta said, breathing deeply and turning her attention back to me with a determination the likes of which I've never seen from her. "When I'm trying to communicate with you, I feel I'm not being heard. I feel I'm being cancelled out. When we get in discussions about this or that, I feel my values are being diminished."

Cancelled out, not heard, values diminished. What is she talking about? I thought to myself.

"I feel you prefer to avoid me rather than have a confrontation. If by chance we do agree on something, somehow you forget it. No matter how positively I try to remind you, we get into an instant cycle of negativity. You will get angry, walk away or do just the opposite of what I need from you."

My God, because I can't get a word in edgewise, I thought. I felt the blood vessels in my neck pulsating.

"It doesn't matter what I say to you; somehow you turn it around the other way, and it now becomes my fault. I'm the unreasonable one. Then the second I have a gut reaction, I'm instantly stereotyped into being hormonal, 'that time of month.' I'm cemented into this pit. You won't talk about it anymore." Leeta stopped abruptly.

"Yeah, Leeta, I walk away to prevent an argument," I said. "When you get going, I can't get a word in edgewise."

"Stop, it's not your time." Jane said firmly.

"Huh?" I responded.

"Not your time," Jane repeated. "Leeta is the speaker and you're the listener. It's your responsibility to understand Leeta *exactly* as she wants to be understood."

"But I disagree."

"It doesn't matter. Does she need to repeat it?" Jane asked flatly.

"No." I was annoyed. "I just disagree."

"Your agreeing or disagreeing isn't the point of this exercise. The only objective is to seek first to understand. Understanding is not agreeing. Easy deep breath," Jane emphatically stated.

"What?"

"Breathe."

"Why?"

"Because you appear to be angry," Jane said calmly. "Breathing, C.J., as you have discovered, will calm you and return you to the front part of your brain."

"Return me to the front part of my brain?"

"Yes, return you to the front part of your brain or your new brain. The moment we become angry, we'll automatically flip into the back part of our brain."

"Flip into the back part of our brain?" Hell yeah, I was angry and getting angrier. *Enough of this psychobabble shit.*

"Yes, and the only thing the back part of our brain or old brain knows to do is to run away or beat up or kill what angers or scares us. With yours and Leeta's loud mean arguments, you beat each other up with your mouths."

"By breathing, I will return to the front part of my brain so I will do . . . do what?"

"Be able to say *exactly* what you want to say in the manner you want to say it and have no regrets. A goal both you and Leeta say you want to accomplish, am I correct?"

"Correct." I looked at Leeta. She had turned away from both Jane and me.

"Are you okay, Leeta?" Jane asked.

"Not exactly; this is what I was afraid would happen. Now he will not talk to me for days."

"You agree with this hallucination about you, C.J.?"

"Hallucination?" Leeta interrupted. Her dark eyes were flashing.

"Yes, hallucination, theory, assumption—that's all it is until you ask C.J. He's the expert about himself, and he's the only one who knows what he feels or thinks right now. Why don't you ask him?"

"Well?" Leeta snapped.

I was knocked for a loop by her retort and carefully responded. "I know what Leeta is talking about. Yes, I haven't talked to you for days, but I didn't know what else to do, to stop the fighting. No, Leeta, I don't like the silence any more than you do. That's why I'm here to learn another way." Leeta stared at me through her dark flashing eyes and did not say a word. I felt my jaw muscles tighten and my teeth clench in response to her penetrating gaze.

"Drop your jaw and breathe easy," Jane instructed me quietly.

I did and as I did, I could feel my heart pounding again in my ears.

"I want both of you to breathe. By now, you know the drill, get yourselves comfortable and close your eyes, good. Now take a deep easy breath in, two, three, four . . ." she repeated in the same slow, even monotone voice as before. "Once again, in . . ."

I could not stay as focused as I had been in the prior session.

"Okay, now slowly open your eyes. How do you feel?"

"It didn't work this time," I responded.

"And you, Leeta?"

"The same."

"We'll do the breathing exercise again until you become calm. Next session, I'll talk more about the importance of breathing, managing anger and staying in the front brain when you two are having a fight."

"I thought one of our goals was not to fight with each other." Leeta responded.

"To stop the mean, loud arguments, yes. However, I worry about couples who say they don't fight, which frequently translates they have become apathetic toward each other. Anything you love is worth fighting for. Another way of saying this is everything we see that's beautiful around us—our mountains, streams, trees, wildlife, and even us—is due to conflict. There is nothing bad about conflict, if you learn how to work with it and not against it. And, once you clearly understand the power of deep breathing to stay calm, and you're committed to stay in the front brain when you're fighting, then we'll pick up in next session where we left off with the speaker-listener exercise with Leeta still being the speaker. Otherwise, your homework is still the same for this week as before, to have fun and not to discuss issues. Agreed?" Jane paused and waited for a response.

"Agreed," I responded, looking over at Leeta. I didn't want a week of silence any more than Leeta did. *"Fun" is good,* I thought, *especially with Thursday being Thanksgiving.*

"Agreed," Leeta said.

"And there's one more assignment to your homework, to do the breathing exercise we have done today for ten minutes twice a day, agreed?"

We both nodded.

"Good," Jane responded quietly. "Get yourselves comfortable, close your eyes and take a deep, easy breath in . . ."

* * *

"C.J.," Leeta said, breaking the silence as we turned into the long, narrow dirt drive that led to the house.

"Yes," I responded quietly.

"I'm going to pick up Travis from school. He should be finishing up Driver's Ed class about now; then we'll run by the grocery store for ice cream for the apple pie I made earlier."

"Okay." That's all I could say. Today's session was the worst yet. I just wasn't prepared for how bad things really were between Leeta and me.

"C.J."

"Huh?"

"Why don't you shower and put on some fresh clothes," she said gently.

"Yeah, good idea. I'll do that." With all the sweating I did in session, I knew I reeked of B.O.

Hannah greeted us as usual, Leeta first and then me. Hannah was definitely a family dog, but her loyalty lay with Leeta. They were always together, either around the barnyard, on the trails behind the house or off in the truck on some errand. If one were seen, the other wouldn't be too far behind. I felt good about that too because I knew Hannah would guard Leeta with her life, if need be.

"Good then, I'll be back in about thirty minutes. Come, Hannah," Leeta commanded as she opened the truck's passenger door for the dog to get in.

I unlocked the kitchen door, turning on the light as I entered. It was five-thirty and already dark. I could smell Leeta's pot roast cooking in the slow cooker, and her apple pie on the counter beside it. Leeta was definitely the queen of slow-cooked meals. The table was already set as usual—a *Currier and Ives* moment as I sat in the rocking chair beside the wood stove in our country kitchen. I got up from the rocker and walked into the den, turning on the table lamp beside the big and welcoming couch. Leeta had the logs stacked in the fireplace ready to be lit. *Tonight will be a good night,* I thought, *to light the fire, taking the chill out of the house and us.* I smiled, thinking about Kate's comment to knock the chill off in and out of the office, when she brought the doughnuts to the plant from McFarlan.

I turned and walked up the stairs to our bedroom. I loved this room. It was our room, the king and queen room. Because of the extensive renovations to the house, it was almost a year before we could tackle the upstairs. We made do with the rooms downstairs, converting them into two bedrooms and a living space, along with the kitchen and the bathroom.

The first night we slept in our bedroom, Leeta lifted her wine glass high into the air and declared, "I hereby proclaim this room to be anointed the king and queen room. No matter what, the king or the queen shall never leave the marital bed." I remembered the ruby red of the wine, glistening from the light of the candles, which adorned every piece of furniture that had a flat surface. I remembered her dark hair spilling over her shoulders, her skin silky soft to my touch and her black onyx eyes sparkling in the candles' yellow, muted light. That night seemed so surreal now, as if it existed only in a fairy tale in a faraway land.

I slumped down on the couch. *When did things go wrong in the marriage? When did we stop talking and started yelling?*

I heard Hannah running up the stairs and Leeta's footsteps followed. I looked down at my watch, six o'clock already. "C.J., are you okay?" Leeta said as she entered our room.

"Yes. Give me about ten minutes, and I'll be downstairs. I haven't showered yet."

"So I noticed, C.J."

"Yes."

"I love you like I've never loved anyone, but the relationship can't stay as it is. Changes need to be made, if we want to make it to the finish line."

"I know, Leeta, I know," I said as Leeta gently closed our bedroom door behind her. I closed my eyes. My heart tightened.

I've heard almost those same words before, except from Cullen: "I will always love you, C.J., forever and a day."

I pleaded, "Please, God, help me get it right this time before I lose her too."

As I finished my plea, a gentle kiss brushed across my cheek and a kind voice whispered into my ear, "You will." I touched my cheek and sat straight up. I could have sworn it was Cullen who kissed me and gave me hope. Or was it God? It was both—Cullen's kiss of forgiveness and God's blessing.

Chapter Ten

Tenacious Kate

"**I**N, TWO, THREE, FOUR AND OUT, TWO, THREE, FOUR," I counted mentally with each inhale and exhale.

"Find a place with a comfortable chair, which has your special things," were Jane's instructions for the ten-minute breathing exercises. "You can trigger a learned conditioned response as the psychologist, Ivan Pavlov, did in his experiment teaching his dogs to salivate by ringing the bell. Your special place will trigger you to calm down and relax, as the ringing bell triggered the dogs to salivate. It's an effective technique to begin the process of quieting down your mind and setting the stage for you to become calm." Well, this was the place, my father's crescent-shaped desk, pictures of Leeta and Travis, and a picture-perfect view outside my window. But the deep breathing just wasn't working like in yesterday's session. Maybe I was trying too hard. Every time I closed my eyes, I saw Leeta's gray pallid face with her dark eyes, deep set and brooding. Twice a day I'm to do this. Damn, I'm struggling to get through just one. I looked at my watch. Only five minutes have gone by.

There were two quick knocks on my office door, but before I was able to okay the knocker's entry, Kate pushed the door open with her backside. Turning around to face me, she pronounced, "This runaway train of unchecked development must be stopped." She was loaded down with her box of holiday decorations, and David followed carrying the bigger box of holiday lights.

Thank you, Kate, I thought. She always came through in my time of need, whether she knew it or not.

"Have you read the *Times-News* this morning?" David asked, placing the box on the floor just inside the door.

"Not yet."

"Well, the county commissioners okayed another mega development. This time it was for 653 units. Robert, Kate and I went to the public comment meeting in Mills River. The meeting was overflowing with the town folk pleading for our county leaders to slow it down. We might as well have stayed home for all the good it did."

"Our agricultural, mountainous community ten years from now will be just a footnote of what Henderson County used to be in some tourist brochure," Kate interjected.

"Seen Robert this morning?" David interrupted.

"No," I responded.

"You know, this new approved development borders his property, and the architectural plans have the cluster homes bordering his backyard. The single family homes will be in another section."

"Jeez," I said quietly.

"There's Robert," Kate said, looking over my shoulder at the picture window behind me.

"Hmm," I said as I swirled my desk chair around.

Robert was walking along the edge of the woods with coffee and newspaper in hand, and then he disappeared into them.

"I want to do things a little differently this year," Kate announced as she cleared her throat.

"What's that?" I asked, still looking out the window at the spot where Robert disappeared. I knew this "runaway train of unchecked development" upset Robert more than the rest of us. As a child in the fifties, he saw his family and life unravel as he watched one orange grove after another be bulldozed for one more cookie-cutter housing development.

"I left Los Angeles as a young man because it was heart-wrenching to see what happened to my hometown," he told me one morning. "As a child, it didn't matter where I stood: orange groves could be seen everywhere. They surrounded the city. By the time I left in the mid-seventies, the orange groves were gone. Families were forced to move out of their neighborhoods and relocate because they could not afford the property taxes. We saw our home bulldozed down in minutes to make room for a more expensive upper-class home. I'll never forget my mother's tears running slowly down her cheeks, as she saw our home crumble into a heaping pile of rubble."

"About the holidays," Kate said, interrupting my memories.

"Yes," I said turning around.

"I want us to decorate the trees with edible goodies for the wildlife. I want to make it a family affair. The employee families can make edible decorations to place on the white pines for the wildlife to eat.

"Huh?"

"Yes, yes," Kate continued excitedly. "You know, like garlands made of popcorn or cranberries or pine cones stuffed with peanut butter and dried fruit." Kate's eyes were glowing. Her cheeks flushed.

"Well, I—"

"We must," Kate again interrupted. "Have you gone into the woods? I saw three whitetail deer just last week. All this development is destroying their natural habitats, and they're coming here."

"Kate, wait a minute. This has to be thought through. We don't want to be biting off more than we can chew. What kind of wildlife would we be inviting here? Robert has seen a bear at his place. And there've been more and more reports of black bear sightings."

"Where's the balance?" Kate asked, crossing her arms.

"Balance," I said slowly, that word again. More and more, I realized it to be the key to almost anything if not everything that exists in our world, at once so simple and yet so complex.

"We need to contact Carolina Mountain Land Conservancy."

"Carolina Mountain Land Conservancy?"

"Yes, they'll assist us in placing the plant's land into a permanent wildlife land trust."

"Kate, wait a minute. I thought we were talking about edible decoration on the white pines. Now you want to set up a permanent wildlife land trust through Carolina Mountain Land Conservancy? That's a big jump. I haven't even agreed on the edible decorations yet."

David didn't open his mouth. He knew Kate as well as I did. Kate's middle name should have been tenacious instead of Elizabeth. She doesn't give up. This tenacity of hers pushed me along in my early years with the plant when I was ready to throw up my hands and close up shop.

Then again, Elizabeth meant queen, so maybe her middle name did fit her. She surely ordered us around, and most of the time, we obeyed.

"Okay then, agreed, that is a big jump. For now, we'll keep it small by taking care of our misplaced wildlife. So what about hanging the edible decorations on the white pines and making it a family affair?" I could hear Kate's foot tapping as it so frequently did, when my answer didn't come as fast as she deemed it should, and from my point of view, one of her less endearing traits.

"After Thanksgiving we'll talk, okay?"

"And that'll be next week when we hang the lights," Kate quipped.

"Lights?"

"Yes, I need help. I'm getting too old to do this by myself. You, David and Robert can help me get them up in no time."

Robert—yes, Robert, I thought to myself as I turned around again to face the large window that stretched across my office back wall. No sight of Robert coming out of the woods sanctuary as I leaned forward in my chair to look more carefully along its boundary. Only two deer walked quietly along the woods' edge and then disappeared into them as Robert had done earlier. "Ah," I heard myself sigh. I was overwhelmed with everything, my marriage, Kate's holiday ambitions, Robert's grief, my lack of focus. The list was long and only getting longer. I prided myself in being the hard ass, the fixer, the poor boy made good. Now I felt I was on that runaway train.

Chapter Eleven

Both Do the Dance

Leeta and I entered Ms. Levy's waiting room. My eye caught the headlines of the *Times-News,* lying on the table between the two chairs facing me. As I sat down, I reached for it and quickly scanned the front page. Another dairy farm sold to a developer for a proposed nine-hundred-home golfing community. I never thought this farmer would sell out. He was one of the dairy farmers working with the North Carolina Agricultural Commission to help save an embattled North Carolina dairy industry.

By April, county planners had already signed off on more subdivision lots than were approved in all of the prior year. We were in a building boom when the rest of the country was slowing down. The newspaper called this surge of new developments the "Big Boom."

The county people complained the unchecked growth affected the surrounding areas by overcrowding schools and overcrowding roads, threatening clean water and electrical supply, storm water run-offs and sewage discharge, flooding, and higher taxes. The list was long. It was sad. The Hendersonville I loved was changing, and I feared not for the best.

"Sorry for interrupting your newspaper time." Jane chuckled. "We can start a little earlier today, my three o'clock cancelled."

Leeta and I both stood up and headed toward our usual chairs. After I sat down I said, "I didn't read the paper this morning, and I was particularly interested in what was last night's vote regarding The Fox Run Golfing and River Community."

"You mean the nine-hundred-home community in Etowah?" Jane responded slowly. Her brows furrowed as she looked away from Leeta and me.

"Yes."

"You know, I moved from Atlanta years ago to escape Atlanta's over development. It took me forty-five minutes every morning and every night to make a ten-mile commute to work. I never knew my neighbors, much less what they looked like. I left in the dark and came home in the dark. Many of Georgia's peach orchards, along with its farmlands have been lost to development over the years. I support growth, but excessive growth with one development after another is not good in my opinion."

Finding the balance, I thought, *easier said than done. What is one person's balance is another person's imbalance.*

"So, how was Thanksgiving?" Jane asked.

"Pleasant," Leeta answered. "There was no silent treatment."

"Good," Jane said as she looked at me. "And you?"

"It was better," I said cautiously.

"I feel C.J. heard what I was saying last time," Leeta continued. "Instead of him rushing to play on his ham radio after work, he looked for Travis and me first. C.J. and I even spent a few nights on the couch in front of the fireplace talking and laughing. This was the man I married who wanted to spend time with me."

No kissing, I thought. *I would have liked that. We used to laugh, talk and kiss on the couch.*

"And you?" Jane asked, turning her attention to me now.

"Yes, I agree with everything Leeta said about our week," I stated awkwardly. I chose not to say that I didn't turn on the ham radio the whole Thanksgiving week-end, nor even go into the room where the radio was. I was intent on doing whatever it took to avert any possibility of an argument.

"C.J., what's going on?"

"What do you mean?" I responded. I knew I didn't want to share what I was thinking. All I have to do is mention the words ham radio, and Leeta would explode. Let me add no sex in over a month and there goes any hope of civility between Leeta and me. *Well, not exactly no sex,* I thought with a quirky smile. *I have taken the matter into my own hand in the shower.*

"Well, you seem preoccupied."

How do I respond? I thought. *Do I lie? I winced at that thought. One thing I don't do is lie. How about omit? Is that a lie? Damn, what's the point of us being here, if I'm afraid to say what I need to say?*

"C.J.?"

"Yes."

"If you don't tell me what's going on, there's no way I can be effective. I'm only as good as the information you give me, remember?"

"Yes, I know." I said looking at Leeta. The red patches had already begun their trek up her neck.

"Well, I'm just not ready to talk about some of my," I stopped, floundering for the right word, "issues."

"That's fine, but as I said to Leeta in our last session, if the issues you're holding back are some of what's causing the tension between you two, they need to be presented."

"They are, but I'm just not ready to talk about them. One thing for sure, we didn't do well talking about our stuff on our own."

"What I'm hearing is you two don't feel safe to share your up close and personal stuff for fear you will upset one another."

"That's it," I said. "We don't feel safe with each other."

"Yes," Leeta said quietly. "Sometimes C.J. explodes so quickly, I don't even know what I've said to upset him."

I rolled my eyes on that one. "And you don't explode, Leeta?"

"Not like you," Leeta responded quickly.

"Stop," Jane said emphatically. "No contest is going to be allowed in this office on who has the bigger anger problem. You're both winners."

The color drained right out of Leeta's face, her jaw tightened, and her lips drew into a tight line across her face.

"You have something to say, Leeta?" Jane asked.

"No," Leeta snapped.

Here we go again, I thought.

"I'm going to repeat this again," Jane said calmly. "You both have participated in the failures in this marriage. It will take both of you to participate in its successes. Blaming is off the table here. Blaming is just a means for someone to get off the hook, so he or she won't have to do anything differently. If allowed, it then becomes the other person's problem and that person's sole responsibility to make the situation better. It won't happen here. In couple's work, it takes two to do the dance." Jane stopped with a look that dared us to challenge her house rules. "Are we okay to continue?"

"Yes," I said. *Good to hear it's both of us and not just me,* I thought. I've forgotten she had said that early on. All I'd been hearing from these sessions is how bad I am, and whatever I do is not good enough.

"Leeta?" Jane asked.

"Yes, I'm okay to continue."

"Good. Last session I introduced the concept of 'Seek first to understand before being understood,' as the first step toward your goal to communicate better. I gave C.J. three tools to use as the listener to aid him in understanding you, Leeta, the speaker, in *exactly* the way you want to be understood. Because of the unmanaged anger both of you exhibited, the speaker-listener exercise wasn't being effective.

"I've already introduced you to deep breathing as a technique to calm down, but I haven't told you why I've been so insistent. In fact, it's mandatory that both of you do it once your initial warning signs of anger have occurred. Any ideas on what they could be for each of you?"

"Sweating," I said. *That has to be a well-known fact by now,* I reflected. *You would have to be blind if you didn't notice.*

"My muscles tighten, my face flushes. I hate when my face turns beet red, but I always do this, even as a child," Leeta revealed.

I'd rather get a red face any day than sweat my guts out, I thought.

"Others?" Jane asked.

"Fast and loud beating heart," I responded.

"Loud?"

"I can hear my heart beat clearly in my ears. I don't hear it any other time, except when I become angry."

"Or scared, possibly, that is if this anger you're emoting is covering up fear. When anyone becomes scared, all his or her senses—sight, sound, smell, touch, taste—are on high alert. Maybe that's why you can hear your heart beat. Any others?"

"Yelling," Leeta said.

"Yes, yelling. But I don't want you to wait to breathe until you are already yelling. I want you to breathe as soon as the voice rises, as with any of the other warning signs you have identified. As soon as you, C.J., feel the heat in your body rise, or the muscles tightening in your jaw, breathe deeply. You, Leeta, as soon as you feel the heat in your neck or muscles tighten, breathe."

She doesn't miss anything, I thought. *She's right. I've already popped one molar by clenching my teeth.*

"Understand?"

We both nodded.

"Leeta, do you feel the heat in your neck now?"

Yep, I thought. *Leeta's neck is already showing small pink patches.*

"Yes."

"Now is the time you do your deep, slow breaths."

"Okay," Leeta said as she breathed deeply.

"Keep in mind that anger can be a cover up for fear, and deep breathing is our best means of managing our anger. Remember, when we become angry, we automatically flip from our front to our back brain. The only way we can flip back into our front brain is to be calm. The good news is our magnificently constructed bodies have a built-in mechanism to return ourselves to this state. It's simply to take deep easy breaths. Herbert Benson, one of the pioneers in mind-body medicine, called this the quieting response. C.J., you've experienced this quieting response a couple of sessions ago, correct?"

"Yes, but I haven't been as successful as I was then."

"You will with practice and patience."

"And, Leeta, you've felt better?"

"Sort of. So the deep breathing allows you to become calm again, and being calm is the only way to return to the front brain." Leeta said this slowly, as if to make sure she understood what Jane was saying. "So being in your front brain is important because why?"

"Good question," Jane answered quickly. "Well, as you know the caveman had no forehead."

We both nodded.

"Man's forehead didn't develop until the cortex or front brain evolved, which happens to be the brain's creative reasoning part. With this development of our new brain, man discovered how to make fire, the wheel, historical records and everything else we have today, which makes our lives so enjoyable, comfortable and convenient and at the same time so destructive and dangerous."

"The double-edged sword," I quipped.

"Yep, depending on choices made, we frequently choose our blessings and our burdens."

"Never thought of it that way," Leeta commented.

"Yes, 'we reap what we sow.' But our getting this concept and making it ours," Jane emphasized as she pointed to her heart, "is empowering."

"Empowering," Leeta repeated.

"Yes, empowering. When you're in the old brain, you can only beat up what you're angered about or afraid of, or you run away. In your case, you two beat each other up with your mouths or you run away."

"I'm not afraid of Leeta," I retorted.

"C.J., I'm not saying you're afraid of Leeta, but what are you afraid of when you allow your anger to control you? Our only authentic feelings are love and fear. But they can morph into other feelings. C.J., the next time you become angry with Leeta, ask yourself what you're afraid of? Your allowing your anger to control you is why you say and do things you don't mean and regret later. This is the only thing the back brain can do."

"Slow, deep breathing returns you to your front brain, so you can talk rationally, instead of staying in your back brain and screaming and yelling at each other," Leeta interjected quietly.

"Yes, Leeta, breathing calms you and returns you to your front brain. Then you're able to have the conversation in which you say *exactly* what you mean with no regrets. The loud, mean arguments are no more," Jane asserted. "Okay then, are we in a good place to pick up where we were in the last session, with Leeta, you being the speaker and C.J., the listener?"

"I'm ready," Leeta responded.

"Me too," I said.

"Reviewing the rules, Leeta, you're to take all the time you need to say what you want. When C.J. repeats your information, it's important that C.J. gets your information *exactly* as you want him to understand you. You need to let him know what is correct and what is not correct.

"C.J., you're clear on your stop tools: information overload, information clarification, and lousy approach?"

"Yes."

"Good. As last time, the conversation is between the two of you, so face each other. I'll cut in as needed to coach you through any hurdles." Jane smiled.

And, I thought, *to breathe.*

Leeta turned to me easily, a big difference from last session. "I frequently feel when I'm talking to you I feel I'm cancelled out, not heard. I frequently feel my values are diminished. If by chance we do reach an agreement, I feel you forget it. If I remind you, we get into an instant cycle of negativity. You get angry, walk away or do just the opposite of what I need from you."

I lifted my hand for Leeta to stop talking. "Do opposite of what you need from me? I don't understand."

"Like the weekend before Thanksgiving, I needed you to nail back fence boards that had fallen down. Instead, you chose to mulch the fallen leaves in the front and back yards. You did a great job, but the leaves could wait. The fences could not. I ended up doing them myself on Monday and Tuesday, which took time away from my paid day job." Leeta paused.

"Is that all you have to say at this time?" Jane asked Leeta.

"Yes."

"Okay. What did you understand Leeta to say, C.J.?"

My palms were clammy. I took a deep breath. "I understood what she said."

Leeta looked at me intently.

"And what did she say?" Jane asked.

"I can't repeat what she said, but I understand."

"No, C.J., you need to repeat what Leeta said, so she knows you understand her information *exactly* as she wants you to understand it."

"I can't repeat it exactly."

"You don't have to *quote* her exactly. You can para-phrase what she said."

"Oh." I was sweating again. I took another deep breath. I looked over at Leeta. Her eyes were pleading.

"Leeta said. . ." I hesitated. "I don't listen to her. I get angry and I walk away."

"Is that correct, Leeta?"

"Well yes and no."

"What do you mean?" Jane asked.

"What he *said* was correct, but I said more."

"Do you know what the more was, C.J.?"

"No." I answered quietly.

"Why?" Jane asked.

"I don't know why."

"Were you being distracted by your own thoughts?"

"I guess. I was disagreeing with her. I wanted to defend myself."

Jane chuckled. "You and everybody else."

"Huh?"

"I'll say it again, you're normal. C.J.; no one is asking you to agree, but to understand. In fact, whether you concur or not is irrelevant because it's Leeta's reality or experience with you, not yours with her. She's giving you a gift by allowing you to understand her world with you."

"Oh." Jane's string of words presented themselves as nice rhetoric, but what she was asking of me was just weird. *It doesn't matter whether I concur with Leeta about me. Leeta's giving me a gift by allowing me to understand her experience with me, even if I disagree with her. It sounds like more psychobabble mumbo jumbo nonsense to me.*

"Leeta, tell C.J. again what you want him to understand, but add nothing extra. You may add more later."

"Okay," Leeta responded.

Leeta faced me again, but this time her eyes were soft and sad. "I feel my values are diminished by you. If we ever do reach an agreement, you frequently forget. When I remind you, we get into a cycle of negativity. You get angry and walk away, or do just the opposite of what I asked you to do."

"Good," Jane said. "What did you understand Leeta to say, C.J.?"

I was unable to look away from Leeta. Her soft brooding dark eyes held me captive. "You feel I diminish your values," I said slowly. "When we do reach an agreement, I forget. When you remind me, I'll get angry and walk away, or do just the opposite of what you have asked." Damn, that was hard to hear about myself, especially since it's Leeta's "reality" with me.

"Is that correct, Leeta?" Jane asked.

"Almost. I said he would *frequently* forget our agreements. He doesn't *always* forget."

Leeta's words resounded loudly inside my head. *Oh, so on a scale of one to ten; with ten being a full-fledged bastard, I am only a nine.*

"Is there any more you want to comment about at this time, Leeta?"

"No."

"C.J., now it is your time."

I looked down. I felt completely defeated. I did nothing right in Leeta's world.

"C.J.?" Jane asked.

"I have nothing to say."

"Why?" Jane asked.

"In Leeta's world, I'm pretty near a full-fledged, hard-assed bastard."

"What? I didn't hear Leeta say you were a bastard."

"Well, close enough. I can't do anything right to please her."

"So that's what going on, you feel everything you do in Leeta's world is wrong."

"That's what I'm hearing. You're not?" I asked sarcastically.

"How about you're both wrong?" Jane said.

"You'll need to convince Leeta of that," I retorted. Leeta said nothing. No way could I look at her. Either those damn red patches would be marching up her face again, or her eyes would be even more brooding.

"Nope, that's not what my role is with you. Instead I'll ask you two, 'What makes something right or wrong?'"

We were both silent. *A good question,* I reflected.

"No takers. Okay then, my definition of right is, if it works, it is right. If it doesn't, it is wrong, as simple as that. And right and wrong is relative too, in that what is right or works for one couple might not be right or work for another." Jane paused and looked at both of us. "Therefore, you're both wrong because you haven't discovered a mutually agreed upon right."

We haven't discovered a mutually agreed upon right, I silently pondered. I sighed. "Well," I mumbled.

"Well what?"

"Finding that mutually agreed upon right between Leeta and me, that's the direction I want us to work on."

"Good, but this is just one of the steps toward Leeta's and your primary goal to stop the loud mean arguments with no resolutions. Practicing deep breathing to control your anger instead of allowing it to control you and practicing the speaker-listener exercise to keep your communication flowing are two more steps toward this goal."

"So C.J., it's your turn to be the speaker and Leeta the listener."

"Yes." I turned toward Leeta, and as I did, Leeta faced me. Her face was not a red mass of red patches, and her eyes were soft. *Okay then,* I reflected, *I'm ready to present my world with you, and it looks that you're ready too.* "Leeta, when you have your mind made up about something, words come out of your mouth like bullets from a rapid-firing Gatling gun. I can't get a word in. I walk away to prevent an argument. You won't give it a rest. You even follow me from room to room until we're having one of our knock-down, drag-out fights. The fights have lasted into the early hours of the morning. By then, I can't even remember what started the fight in the first place or what we were fighting about. All I remember is all the ways I make you unhappy. Do I do anything right? Anything?" By the end, my voice had become quite loud. My attempt to stay calm had dissipated.

"Thank you, C.J.," Jane said calmly. "What do you both need to do first, before Leeta repeats back what you've said?"

"Breathe." We both said in unison.

* * *

"C.J.," Leeta said quietly on the way home.
"Yes."

"I'm sorry."

"For what," I replied.

"I understand now why you walk away from me. So words come out of my mouth like a Gatling gun?" Leeta said.

I turned and faced her. Her black eyes were smiling.

"I guess the fieriness of my Black Irish ancestry comes through a wee bit at times," Leeta said feigning an Irish brogue as she gently touched my face.

I took a deep breath and exhaled quietly. *If she only knew her power over me . . .*

Chapter Twelve

Decorating for Christmas

BREATHE IN, TWO, THREE, FOUR AND OUT, TWO, THREE, FOUR; my breathing was light and effortless. Beyond all reason, I felt I was floating slightly above my chair. A subdued energy cradled me. This feeling had never happened before, but I knew I was completely safe. The phrase, "Become aware of your surroundings," entered into my mind. I felt myself float down to my chair. My arms rested comfortably beside me. I heard a soft tap on the door. It was Kate. For the past week, twice a day, the routine was for her to knock on my door after ten minutes and allow no interruptions. I breathed in deeply and slowly opened my eyes. I took Ms. Levy's advice to practice and be patient. Today's exercise was close to the peace I had felt in her office a few weeks back. The floating sensation was indeed extraordinary. So, this is meditation, and the tough guy is doing it.

I looked out my window at the grayish-white, cloud-covered sky. A wind was blowing the tops of the now-barren trees. There was a winter snow advisory for the Western North Carolina mountains by late afternoon. I wondered if the forecast had changed to a winter watch.

I heard Kate and David talking; then Leeta's laughter. I didn't remember Leeta saying she was coming to the plant today. I heard chairs and tables being moved. *What's going on?* I opened my office door.

Leeta stood in front of me smiling. "Hi, soup's on." She placed her crock-pot on a long table, which had been placed in the center of the waiting area. She reached into a grocery bag, took out two fresh loaves of bread and then brought the bread up to her nose and sniffed. "Yum, I like nothing better than Underground Bakery's French sourdough bread with a bowl of homemade split pea soup. How about a cup? New recipe from Ina."

Before I could respond, Kate appeared from her office with two pumpkin pies.

"My favorite pie." Kate chuckled. "Pie, pie, I love pie."

Robert walked in with Alice. "Vegetarian chili any-one?" he asked.

"Alice," I blurted.

"Hello, C.J.," she said calmly. "Good to see you."

The employees from the machine room began walking in with their wives and girlfriends. They each brought with them a food dish and placed it on the long table beside Leeta's pea soup from Ina (whoever she was), Robert's chili and Kate's pumpkin pies. Soon the table was a cornucopia of food. There were steaming hot stews and casseroles alongside pies, cookies and brownies.

"Oops, we need drinks," Kate announced. "C.J., please help me get some cool drinks from the employee's lounge."

Without saying a word, I followed obediently. "Have I missed something?" I finally asked, entering the employees' lounge. "Somebody getting married, having a baby, what?"

"Oh nothing like that. We're decorating for the holidays, remember?"

I was annoyed. "Remember what?"

"That I needed help with putting up the Christmas lights and decorations this year. I was getting too old to do it by myself."

"Yes, I remember that part. How much decorating are we doing? I mean, do we need every employee we have and their spouses or friends to help?"

"Yes, and their children when school lets out at three o'clock," Kate said calmly.

"Their children, for what?" I could feel the heat rising in my chest.

"To help make edible decorations for the small white pines."

"Kate, I never agreed to that." My voice was rising. "I said we would talk about it after Thanksgiving."

"C.J., you're raising your voice. This is a good time for you to breathe."

"What?"

"That's what you told me the ten-minute breathing exercises were for, to stay calm and relax when you get upset. This is one of those times."

Kate was right. This was a good time. I sat down in a chair while Kate retrieved drinks from the lounge's refrigerator and placed them in a plastic red crate. One of the perks we gave to our employees was free sodas, and Kate kept the bottom two shelves of the refrigerator well stocked.

When she finished filling two plastic crates full of drinks, she sat in a chair that faced me. "Yes, C.J., you did say we'll discuss putting edible decorations on the white pines after Thanksgiving. I understood your concern about encouraging black bears to the plant if we did this. I took the liberty to talk to Robert. He agreed with you, but also he felt it was a great idea. You have a hundred acres of woods that border undeveloped private land in the Green River area that, in turn, border Dupont State Forest. Robert felt we could keep Winnie the Pooh safely at bay if we hung our edible goodies deep in the woods. And, he said bear sightings are very rare during the winter months because they hibernate. The edible goodies we hang will mostly be enjoyed by the deer, birds, raccoons, foxes and squirrels."

"Okay," I said.

"That's it, no comment?" Kate asked.

"Well, yes, I do want to make a comment. You know we are right in the middle of bear country." I asserted.

"Yes."

"You remember last May when a Henderson County home-owner killed a black bear in his back yard?"

"The man who was awakened by his dog barking. When he got up, he found a bear standing on his hind legs threatening his dog. He got his shotgun and wounded the bear and then followed him into the woods and killed him." Kate responded.

"Correct. You know why that happened, don't you?"

"Because we're encroaching on the bears' land."

"Kate."

"They were here first."

"Kate."

"I know, I know. Most bear-human encounters are due to food left outside our homes. But we will do it only in the months of December and January, way before the bears start looking for spring food supplies."

"Kate."

"C.J."

"I thought this was just during the holiday season. You've added another month."

"So."

"Okay."

Kate chuckled.

"What?" I asked.

"This breathing, it works. Maybe we should make breathing for ten minutes twice a day mandatory for everyone."

*   *   *

The snow started slowly at five o'clock and quickened its pace by five-thirty. Families were urged to go home before the roads became treacherous. Travis had called his mother at four-thirty saying his Driver Ed class was cancelled, and one of the other students' parents would take him home. By six-thirty, a light blanket of snow had already covered the ground, trees and gravel drive. "We need to be going, all of us, before we can't," I said to David, Kate, Robert and Alice.

"You're right," Kate said. "We can finish storing the tables and chairs tomorrow."

"Maybe, if this snow keeps coming down as fast as it is now and continues through the night as the weather channel predicts, the plant will be closed," I responded. I went to get Leeta's truck from the back parking lot to pick her up at the plant's front door. My trusty old Volvo wasn't the car to be driven on snowy roads.

"Bye, Kate. It was great fun. This needs to become a holiday tradition," Leeta yelled as she opened the truck's back door and placed her crock-pot and the grocery bag filled with leftover goodies on the truck's floor. She opened up the front door and hopped in.

Leeta's cheeks were rosy red and her hair damp from the falling snow. She was as agile as any twenty-something. No one would ever know she was forty years old.

"It was great fun wasn't it, C.J.?"

"Yes--"

"The kids did a great job," Leeta broke in, "stringing the popcorn garlands and making the pine cone ornaments stuffed with that peanut butter bird seed goop Kate concocted. I bet there isn't one pine cone left on the forest floor. Robert must've picked up every one of them."

"Yeah, I bet he did," I responded.

"The white pines looked lovely all dressed up. Look, a buck. There's a doe, too." Leeta whispered.

We both were quiet as we slowly drove by. The animals looked at us intently before they went into the woods.

"They didn't seem scared," Leeta remarked.

"No, they didn't."

"They know we're looking after them," she said.

I smiled as I looked over at her. The snow fell softly onto the truck's windshield. All that was heard was the whooshing of the wipers. We both were silent on the way home as we took in the beauty of the snow-covered roads and trees. The lights of homes were showing through the trees. There were only a few cars on the road now as more of the town folk were settling in for a wintry night. When I turned into our driveway, I could see the house all lit up. I parked the truck outside the kitchen door. Hannah ran toward the truck, barking and wagging her tail, and as I opened the truck door, a snowball splattered onto my chest.

"Snowball fight!" Travis cried out.

"You're on, son!"

Chapter Thirteen
Snow Day

THE PHONE RANG. I LOOKED AT THE DIGITAL CLOCK ON THE bedside table: six-thirty in the morning, an hour past my usual wake up time. I reached across Leeta's side of the bed to answer the phone. She wasn't there. "Just a minute, Kate, I'll get him," I heard Leeta say from the hall phone down stairs.

I turned on the bedside lamp, took the remote and turned on the television to the early morning local news channel.

"Well, folks, if you're just waking up, you're waking up to six inches of snow, and it's still coming down at a record pace," the weather girl announced. "We have a wintry snow watch until midnight. Buncombe, Henderson and Transylvania counties, no school for you today, have a great snow day. Look across the bottom of your television screen for more closings of schools and businesses."

Leeta walked into our bedroom. "Kate's on the phone, wants to know about closing the plant."

"Hello, Kate," I said, picking up the phone. "Yep, sure do. Call WHKP Radio Station and WLOS-TV. We'll talk tonight about tomorrow. Thanks Kate, goodbye."

"Where did you go?" I asked as Leeta crawled into bed beside me.

"To let Hannah out. She nudged me with that cold wet nose of hers."

I laughed. "Got you up instead of me this time, good for her."

"Well, you're it next time," Leeta said, turning off the bedside lamp and then curling up to me. "We can sleep in today, no school and no work. I've already checked on the horses and threw some hay into each stall."

"Sounds good to me," I said and pulled her in closer to warm her chilled body. She easily folded into me. Leeta took my top arm and wrapped it around her waist. Her sweet, fresh-smelling hair brushed softly against my chin. I felt her chest lift up and fall in. She was already asleep. I closed my eyes, and I, too, fell asleep in the comfort of our bed with my queen in my arms.

* * *

Eight o'clock, the digital clock read as I opened my eyes. Neither Leeta nor I had moved from our positions. I could hear the snow softly hit our tin roof. I took in a deep breath to enjoy this moment of complete tranquility.

"Breakfast?" Leeta said as she rolled over facing me, propping herself up on her right arm.

"Sounds good to me."

"And the three of us go on a horseback ride through town afterward?"

"Sure."

"Hannah can come too. I'm sure the roads we travel will be free of traffic."

"It sounds like a plan. What can I do to help?"

Leeta smiled as she sat up, arched her back, extended both her arms outward into a stretch and yawned. "Well, since you asked . . ." She looked at me sheepishly. "You can get Travis up, and you two can see to the horses. They need for you to feed them their grain, fill their water buckets and muck their stalls."

"Oh my," I said.

Leeta laughed as she leaned over and gave me a quick kiss. "And the horses need to be blanketed and let out. My king and my young prince will be duly rewarded with a breakfast fit only for royalty."

"But kings and princes don't muck stalls, it's the servants' job," I said uneasily.

"Ah, so true, my lord, but as you can tell, the deep treacherous snow has prevented them from leaving their homes."

The telephone rang. Leeta answered it. "Hello, Jane. No problem. Yes, we'll look at our schedule and call tomorrow to reschedule for this week. Oh sure, definitely next Tuesday at our normal time. Enjoy your day too."

Already I'd bounced out of bed, opened the shutters and looked out the window. The house, barn and pasture surrounded by several acres of woods were completely blanketed with a thick layer of pristine snow. We had our own wintry wonderland smack in the middle of Hendersonville.

When I turned around, Leeta had already vanished into the bathroom. I went to Travis's room where he was sitting on the edge of his bed putting on his winter boots. "Up and dressed already," I stated.

"Yeah, I heard Mom say, we're the stable guys today, and after breakfast, she wants to go on a horseback ride through town."

"You okay with that?"

"Sure. Mom has always been one to make a big deal out of a snow day. I bet today she'll fix a country breakfast complete with homemade biscuits and Mr. Collins's honey. Maybe she'll slice some of that country ham she brought from Bat Cave just before Thanksgiving."

I asked, "How long is it going to take us to do everything?"

"An hour at the least. I've got to eat a bowl of Cheerios to tide me over. I'm starving." Travis grabbed his coat and toboggan off the hook from the back of his bedroom door and skirted past me.

I returned to our bedroom. I've never been part of the upkeep of the horses, and mucking stalls was something I never wanted to do. Nasty was the only word I could think of to describe the chore. Getting the horse ready to ride—like brushing and saddling—was one thing, but this mucking, blanketing, feeding, that was something else. "Ahhh," I sighed as I opened my shirt drawer and put on a heavy long sleeve shirt over my undershirt. I pulled on one of my two pairs of long johns, took my jeans off my clothes rack from where I hung them last night and pulled them on, then my socks and shoes. Now a sweater. I opened the cedar chest at the foot of the bed. I pulled the sweater over my head, pushing my arms through the sweater's sleeves as I reluctantly went down the back steps, which led to the kitchen. Travis was already eating his cereal, and the coffee maker was halfway through its drip cycle. The flour and milk were on the counter for the biscuits, and the ham was sitting on the chopping block ready to be trimmed. My stomach was growling.

Leeta reached for the measuring cups from the cabinet. Some stray hairs had already escaped her barrette, falling onto the collar of her fleece bathrobe. She had on the Eskimo bedroom slippers her father gave her when she was sixteen. Leeta was sentimental about the littlest things. I would've loved to have scooped her up into a big hug, but I still didn't feel free to be spontaneous. I'd stopped counting the days since we had sex. This morning was the first time I felt safe to pull her close, because she curled into me first.

"Coffee's ready," Leeta said as she poured the coffee into a thermos and tightened the top.

Taking the thermos, I asked, "Well, Travis, ready?"

"Yep, ready."

Hannah was already outside barking for us to come out. I had to laugh, seeing her coat with tiny snowballs covering her legs, belly and wagging tail. Travis threw her a snowball that promptly crumbled in her mouth and fell in tiny pieces to the ground. She tried in vain to pick the vanishing ball up with her teeth.

"Silly dog," Travis said, giving Hannah a big hug.

This is what makes living worthwhile, I thought, as the king and the prince with their trusted dog walked steadfastly to the stables to muck the stalls and feed the royal horses and then be rewarded by our queen with a breakfast fit for a king and a prince for a job well done.

* * *

"Isn't this great riding through town on horseback? So beautiful and quiet. I love the sound of falling snow. It's just so . . ." Leeta paused, curling her nose as she thought of the perfect word. "Peaceful. Yes, peaceful."

"Yeah," I responded through chattering teeth. We had just turned onto Fifth Avenue, which ran perpendicular into Hendersonville's Main Street. Every rooftop, tree, bush and everything else, including us, were covered with snow. Because it was still snowing hard, there were no children outside building snowmen or even sledding. They were all inside keeping warm, where we should be.

"Lucky too, that the roads haven't been scraped. It keeps the cars off the road," Leeta rattled on. "And look at Tezir, that's one happy horse." Travis and Tezir were a block ahead of us and walking at a fast clip.

"She is?" It was incredulous to me that anyone, even including a horse, could be happy being in this frigid weather.

"Sure is. Look at her tail. It's raised high and switching back and forth. Charlie is enjoying it too. He's in no hurry. See how relaxed he is with his stretched out neck."

"Really?" Charlie's head was as low as it could possibly go without having his nose scrape the ground. He looked like I felt, miserable and cold.

Hannah, her tail wagging, barked and ran ahead of us to catch Travis and Tezir. Leeta laughed, "Guess we're too slow for her."

I looked over at her and Ajax. Ajax held his head high, and he rounded his neck at its poll. His long black mane covered his whole neck, stopping at his shoulder line. His ears were standing straight up, but they kept turning intermittently toward his lady. *Damn horse, he is completely focused and attentive to her, awaiting her next command, like me. Damn horse.*

Travis stopped and turned around to face us.

"Everything okay, son?" Leeta hollered.

"I'm fine. We need to walk Main Street together."

"Why?"

"You'll see."

As we turned onto the tree-lined street, every tree for ten blocks was lit and decorated with holiday splendor. Not a word was spoken as we rode our horses down the center of Main Street. In all of downtown, it was just our horses, our dog and us. It was beautiful . . . magical . . . peaceful and . . . COLD!

*　*　*

"Hot chocolate and marshmallows, fellas?"

"Sure," Travis said. "Any of those brownies left from yesterday's decorating party at the plant?"

"Yep, and chocolate chip cookies too."

"Coats, shoes, wet whatevers in the mudroom, you two," Leeta said, peeling off her coat and hat as she headed toward the designated room for the wet "whatevers." Travis and I followed her, per instructions.

Travis pulled off his boots. "I'm freezing and wet. I've got to take a hot shower. I can't stop shaking."

"Well, don't forget to bring the rest of your wet stuff downstairs," I said, following him. I stopped abruptly in front of the doorway of the small office where my ham radio resided on the desktop. It felt like months since I had sat at the desk chair with my fingers gently touching the ham key as I tapped out my words. I felt like a kid pressing his nose against the closed, candy store window. I heard Leeta taking dishes out of the kitchen cupboard, and I jumped backward from the door. Now I felt like a kid caught with his hand in the cookie jar. *Damn,* I thought, *this is ridiculous.*

"C.J.," Leeta called.

"Yes,"

"We need wood for the stove in the kitchen. Would you bring some dry wood from the side porch?"

"Sure," I said walking back toward the kitchen. She had set the kitchen table with mugs and plates. The brownies and cookies graced the center of the table, along with a bowl of red grapes.

"I've got a great hot chocolate recipe from Ina that I want to make."

"Ina?"

"You know, Ina, the Barefoot Contessa."

"Oh, yes, that Ina," I said, pretending to know who or what she was even talking about as I walked to the mudroom to retrieve my muckers, then back out the kitchen door onto the side porch. Using Jane Levy's words, I was feeling a little off-balance with my personal time. I passed the office's window and saw my ham radio again. *Horseback riding in the cold, wet snow and mucking stalls, ugh.* A great snow day for me would've been a morning play period with Leeta and capping it off with her country breakfast, then letting my breakfast settle by tapping out Morse code with my new Italian bug. I was okay with the snow ride on horseback once it had stopped snowing, but not before. Hot chocolate and brownies afterward; then I'm in front of my ham radio catching up on radio chatter. In the evening, I'm enjoying a glass of wine with Leeta in front of the fireplace with a romp in the king and queen bed later. Now that's a snowy day retreat.

Leeta opened the back door and let Hannah out, which interrupted my daydream, "Take Hannah with you, please."

"Hey, girl, aren't you tired yet?" I said, giving her a pat. *Guess not,* I thought. Goldens were known for their joy of running and retrieving. They will go and go until the owner says 'that's it,' and Hannah was no different. "Here, girl, take this to Leeta," I said, handing Hannah a piece of kindling wood. I picked up an armful of wood from the woodpile and headed toward the kitchen. Travis opened the door as we approached it.

"Mom has gone upstairs to take a quick shower, she says."

I smiled. "Hey, Travis, how about you stoking the fire and putting the wood in the stove while I take off the rest of my wet clothes and get some dry ones on."

"Sure."

Great. My chance to make a few contacts. I hurriedly took my wet clothes off and dashed up the back stairs to put on dry ones. Leeta was not known for a quick shower. By my calculations, I had a good hour.

Dressed and back downstairs, I flipped the switch on my ham radio, and its dial immediately began to glow. I eased into my desk chair. Seconds later, the speaker began to give forth the comforting sounds of Morse code. It was relaxing to tune across the band and listen to the activity. Stations from all over the USA, and sometimes the world, were right there in this small room.

Whoa, what was that? I wondered. Tuning carefully back across the signal, I heard the dahs and dits of ZL4XS tapping out CQ, CQ, CQ. The signal was not strong, but it was steady, and I could easily make it out

. . . NEW ZEALAND. That was a new one for me—never had worked New Zealand on any band. He probably was running high power and my 100-watt Ten Tec Omni Seven might not be up to the task, but I sure wanted to try it. Listening carefully, I could still hear the shower upstairs. I began sending first his call and then my own. When done, I listened carefully. Would I be lucky? Yes, there he was responding to my call. He gave me a 539 signal report, weak but readable. He was in Riverton, New Zealand, and his name was Harry. I gave him a 559 signal report and told him of our location and my name. I then told him of our snowstorm and how lovely and quiet it was. He was amused; it was summertime down there, and snow was far from his mind. I was enjoying his steady hand and well-formed code.

My joy was abruptly halted by a rustling sound from outside the office door. No, it couldn't be. I turned slowly in the direction of the sound. There stood Leeta. She had on her fleece bathrobe and Eskimo slippers. She stood in the doorway, not saying a word and then walked away.

Oh hell, caught with my hand in the cookie jar. I looked down at my watch. It had been only thirty minutes since Travis told me Leeta had gone to take a "quick shower." *Damn, the one time I would've loved for her to have taken her long shower.* I told Harry that I had to QRT, ham talk for shut down my station. I quickly signed off, flipped the power switch and watched the dial dim and go out. I sat in the dimly lit room and stared at the now-dead radio. I heard no sounds coming from the kitchen. I heard muted music coming from Travis's room. I felt guilty. Why? I had done nothing wrong. I got up from my chair and headed toward the kitchen. It was dark. I turned on the light. The table was still set with its treats. *Now what?* I thought. *Do I go find her? For what? Jeez.*

I heard Hannah slowly walking toward the kitchen. I turned toward the dining room door, and there stood

Travis with Hannah standing beside him, wagging her tail. Would I love Hannah's life, to be in such bliss.

"Mom said for us to fend for ourselves, ham and biscuits and pea soup in the frig."

"Hmm, that's fine."

"You got on the radio?"

"Yeah, I did."

"Hmm."

"What? I haven't been on the damn thing for weeks!"

"It's a snow day."

"What does that mean?"

"For Mom, they're special, that's all."

Chapter Fourteen
When's *My* Time?

LEETA DID NOT COME DOWNSTAIRS AGAIN AFTER SHE CAUGHT ME operating the ham radio. Travis and I ate a quiet supper together of soup and ham biscuits. We made hot chocolate from a packet and ate cookies and brownies in front of the fire. We said little. He reviewed for a test, and I read a book. Around ten, Travis went upstairs to go to bed, and I heard him wish his mother goodnight. I sat by the fire until almost midnight before climbing the stairs to our bedroom. Leeta had left my dresser lamp on. She appeared to be asleep and curled up tightly on her side of the bed. We promised never to leave the marital bed, but she might as well be in another room. *Damn the king size bed, I hate them.*

When I woke up, Leeta already was up, and Hannah was gone from her bed too. I passed by Travis's room. He was still sleeping, another snow day for him. Leeta was not in the kitchen, but the coffee was made. I looked out the window and saw Leeta and Hannah heading toward the barn. I thought about walking down the drive to see if the *Times-News* had arrived, and opted not to. I ate a bowl of Cheerios and heated up a ham biscuit. I sat in silence. The contrast from yesterday to today was surreal.

I left a note on the counter beside the coffee pot:

I'm going to the plant to check on things, and taking the truck.

Robert had called, saying he scraped the road to the plant and the parking lot with his bulldozer. As I drove cautiously toward the plant, I recalled when Robert first bought his exorbitant toy. Upon my questioning his purchase, he declared, "It'll save me money in the long run with the clearing of my land and pay for itself ten times over by my renting it out or folks hiring me to do odd jobs." The snow scraping for the plant became one of his paid odd jobs.

Kate's car was parked in her space. I knew Kate would come in once Robert had cleared the drive and parking lot, even though the decision was to close the plant another day. I parked in the parking space marked,

C.J. Alfred, President.

I took a deep breath and let out a loud sigh. At least Leeta and I weren't into one of our loud, mean arguments. Was this better?

*   *   *

There was a soft knock on my office door, and then the door opened gently.

"C.J.," Kate whispered.

"Yes."

"It's been ten minutes. And Leeta called . . . wants you to call her when you've finished your breathing exercise."

"Thanks." My ten-minute breathing exercise didn't work. It was impossible to stay focused. My mind was running haywire with thoughts of Leeta. I was overwhelmed with what she required from me to be happily married.

"How long do you plan on staying?" Kate asked, interrupting my thoughts.

"Oh, I don't know."

"I plan to leave around the noon hour," Kate announced. "It's still in the low thirties and nothing's really thawing out."

"Okay." Kate closed the door softly. I took a deep breath in and let it out in a loud sigh.

I looked at the phone. I didn't want to have a discussion about yesterday. What's the point anyway? Being married to Leeta was becoming quite clear to me, no life outside of her. Was this okay for me? I took a deep breath and let out another sigh. I reached for my cell and pressed eight, the home number.

"Hello," Leeta said.

"Kate said you called."

"Jane said she would see us today at two."

"Okay."

"Okay what?"

"Okay to seeing Jane at two. I'll need to pick you up. I have the truck."

"Yes, I know. On the way, Travis wants to be dropped off at Hendersonville Middle Grade to go sledding with his friends for the hour we are in session."

"I'll be at the house around 1:30."

"Thank you," Leeta said.

"Sure. Goodbye." I got up from my chair and took my coat and hat from the coat rack that graced my sidewall near my office door. Robert had made the rack out of deer antlers from Smiley's Flea Market in Fletcher. He was no hunter, but he said he couldn't pass them up. Kate was not in her office, and I assumed she had already left for the day. It wasn't quite noon. I walked through the machine room and out the back door. I took in a deep breath. There was no breeze, and the cold felt invigorating. I continued to take deep breaths as I headed for the woods. I needed to rid myself of the sickening apathy filtering through my body. As I entered the woods, I found myself sheltered by the snow-capped trees. The only noise I heard was the soft crunch of snow as I walked toward a log bench that faced the snow-covered Blue Ridge Mountains encased in the cloudless blue sky. I sat down, closed my eyes and again took a deep breath. I took in the cold through my nostrils deep into my chest and blew loudly the "bad" air out my mouth. With each breath, I forced out the apathy that was poisoning my soul. I felt myself becoming lighter and lighter with each breath. I felt the sun shine its warmth on my face and my ungloved hands. I lifted my face up for the sunlight to massage my furrowed brow and soften the pain that was pounding in my head. The energy around me slowed itself into a peaceful gait. I felt a feather-like touch brush across my cheek, not unlike what I felt a couple of weeks ago. I touched my cheek with my fingers, and as I did, a gentle but strong voice whispered into my ear, "C.J., you will make it all the way to the finish line. Just show up and be there."

I heard my own voice. "I will, and thank you for being at my shoulder." I lowered my head, opened my eyes slowly, and I drank in all of nature's abundant beauty. I took in a deep relaxing breath. My headache was gone. The hollowness I had been feeling was gone. I looked down at my watch. It was one o'clock. "I'm good," I said to myself as I headed toward the parking lot.

*　*　*

Hannah was standing at the end of the drive, barking and wagging her tail. She bounded toward me as I opened the truck's door. Her coat was covered again with tiny snowballs. Travis was walking up the hill with his sled, and he too, was covered from head to toe with snow.

"What happened?"

"I crashed into a snow bank at the bottom of the hill."

"Are you okay?"

"Sure," he grinned. "I'll need to put on some dry clothes before I go to Middle Grade.

"Where's your mother?"

"She's coming."

No sooner had I said that, Leeta walked up the same hill and was as snow covered as Travis.

"What happened to you?"

She laughed, "The same thing that happened to Travis. I collided into the snow bank at the end of the hill. I'm getting too old for this."

I thought, *No she isn't.* She had on a ski suit covering her clothes and one of those tight fitting wool hats covering her head. Her cheeks were a bright rosy red from the cold, and as usual, hair tendrils were escaping from underneath her hat.

"Let me get my wet stuff off and put on another coat before we leave."

Leeta headed toward the house. Travis had already gone in, leaving Hannah and me standing outside by ourselves. "Well, girl, let me dry you off and see if I can pluck some of those snowballs from your coat."

"Thanks for rubbing Hannah down," Leeta said as she got into the truck. Travis was already in the back seat and had put his sledding gear in the back of the truck. Hannah was locked safely in the kitchen with her dog bed in front of the wood stove. Before we left, Hannah pleaded with her big brown eyes to go with us. When she was told she was to "stay," she curled herself up reluctantly on her bed. "You're our Golden Retriever killer dog, protector of the house," Leeta said, giving Hannah a gentle pet on her head.

I looked at Leeta. She was smiling at me. *What is going on? Did last night even happen?*

* * *

"Hello," Jane Levy said, greeting us in the waiting room when we entered. She had on jeans, a big turtleneck sweater that besieged her small frame and heavy snow boots covered with snow. Her hair was curlier than usual, her cheeks were a bright red, and her moss green eyes were brilliant in color. I again wondered how old she was. By looking at the dates of her degrees on her wall, I calculated she had to be closing in on sixty, if not already, but that seemed impossible.

"You walked?" I asked.

"Yes," she laughed. "I live on Fifth. It's a short walk for me. I'm a Georgia gal too. Snow is not something I'm used to driving in, but I don't mind walking in the snow."

Jane extended her arm toward the therapy room. "Let's get started."

"Okay then, Leeta, you called wanting an appointment as soon as possible. So who wants to begin?" Jane asked once we were all seated.

"I guess I do since I made the appointment, but if C.J. wants to begin, that's fine too." Leeta looked at me.

"No, you go first." I needed to hear what her issues were. *She's the one who got in a huff, not me,* I mused.

"Well, yesterday, we as a family were having a lovely day together. I love snow days in which the world stops its normal routine. For me, it's a priceless opportunity to get off the merry-go-round of life and enjoy just being with each other. Travis knows this about me. These kinds of days are the memory makers, not just for Travis, but for C.J. and me as well. This was the first time in our five years of marriage, C.J., you appeared to want to do this with us.

In the past, when schools and businesses shut down because of the weather, you didn't shut down. You got up at your usual time, went to work, stayed gone most of the day and came home, rushing first to check your ham radio mail. Instead, this time you slept in, something you don't do even on weekends. You were receptive to my suggestions on how I would like to spend the day. You asked what you could do to help. You agreed to muck the stalls and feed the horses with Travis, and you were a good sport about it. Mucking the stalls is something I know you dislike immensely. I thought finally, there is hope that you will make other priorities in your life, other than your work and the plant."

Jane held her hand up, looked at me and asked, "Does Leeta need to stop?"

"No," I responded.

"Remember, you're responsible for the information."

"I know." Frankly, I didn't know whether I could remember everything Leeta was saying. I did agree with what she was saying about the improved me, but she still didn't explain her flap about my being on the ham radio.

Jane nodded to Leeta to continue.

"We went horseback riding in the snow. When we returned to the house, we were wet and cold. I offered to make homemade hot chocolate to warm everybody up, but first I needed a hot shower. I was freezing. C.J. was outside getting wood. I told Travis to tell C.J. I was going to take a quick shower. I know I was back downstairs—twenty minutes, thirty tops. C.J. was already tapping away on his radio. I felt betrayed, scared . . . I guess both. Were his changes sincere? Were they going to last? I've got to be assured by C.J. that the changes he is making now will be equally as good in the future." Leeta stopped.

Jane asked, "Is there more?"

"No more, well, yes, I went upstairs and C.J. stayed downstairs for the rest of the day and evening."

"C.J., what did Leeta say."

Jeez, I am amazingly calm, I reflected. The breathing does help. "I heard Leeta say snow days are memory makers for her, a time when normal routine is stopped and families can take the time to enjoy each other. Usually, when businesses and schools closed for bad weather, my routine of getting up early, going to work and making contacts on the radio didn't stop. This is the first time I showed any interest in enjoying the day with Leeta and Travis." I took a deep breath and exhaled gently as I deliberated on what else Leeta said. "And she said I asked what I could do to help, and I even cleaned the stalls with Travis. She was hopeful that I made other priorities in my life other than work and the plant. When she caught me on the radio, she felt betrayed and scared. Were my changes genuine and were they going to last?" I paused and took another deep breath with an easy release.

"Is there more?" Jane asked quietly.

"Yes, one more thing, the rest of the day and evening we had nothing more to do with each other."

"Is that correct?" Jane asked Leeta.

"Yes," Leeta said, looking directly at me. Amazingly, no red patches were marching up her neck. Then again, I wasn't sweating.

"Is there more you want to say, Leeta?"

"No."

"Okay, C.J., your turn to be speaker."

"Well, everything you said about yesterday I agreed with. I will assure you the changes you see in me are genuine, and they're going to last and be equally as good. However, I'm feeling really off balance with *my* time to myself. It's been weeks since I've turned on the ham radio to avoid any arguments. Yesterday, I spent the day doing what you wanted to do. Most of it I enjoyed, but I need some time to do what *I* enjoy, and making contact on the radio is one of them. You were taking a shower when I signed on, and I planned to sign off as soon as you were done. You didn't even give me a chance to show you. You immediately thought the worse of me." I looked directly at Leeta when I said this, and she at me with no red patches or brooding eyes. *What is happening?*

"Is there more?" Jane asked.

"No, that's all."

"Leeta?"

"I heard C.J. say that he assures me his changes are genuine, and they're going to last. He's feeling really off balance with time to himself. He hasn't been on the ham radio in weeks to avoid any arguments between us. He needs time doing what he enjoys. He planned to sign off as soon as I finished my shower. I immediately thought the worse of him and didn't give him the opportunity to show me."

"Is that correct?" Jane asked me.

"Yes."

"Hmm, there's one more point that wasn't mentioned," Jane continued. "As I've said, I assume everything a person says is important or they wouldn't say it. C.J., you also said you spent yesterday doing what Leeta wanted and most of it you enjoyed. Is that important for Leeta to know?"

"Yes."

"Leeta, do you remember that point?"

"Yes."

"Is there more you want to say, C.J.?"

"No."

"Leeta, it's your turn to be speaker."

Leeta didn't respond immediately. She took a deep breath and released it. She turned toward me and began slowly. "I guess I need to ask a clarification question. I knew cleaning the stalls was something you didn't like doing because you've been very clear about that the past few times you've helped me. But what else don't you enjoy?"

"Well." I paused. "Riding through town on the horses was fun and beautiful, but I would've chosen a time when it had stopped snowing. But I understood riding in the snow was something *you* really enjoyed, so I didn't object."

"Leeta, what did you hear C.J. say?" Jane asked.

"I heard him say riding through town on the horses was fun and beautiful, but he would have chosen a time when it wasn't snowing."

"Is that correct, C.J.?"

"Yes, but I said more. I also understood Leeta really enjoyed riding in the snow, so I didn't object."

"And you didn't like it," Leeta interrupted.

"Not exactly. I enjoyed riding through town. I would have preferred doing it in drier weather, that's all." I was beginning to sweat.

"Breathe," Jane interrupted. "We'll not continue until your voices are lowered. Leeta, your neck is reddening; breathe until that's averted. C.J., get stabilized whatever is overworking inside you. You both close your eyes and breathe."

I closed my eyes and methodically began the breathing exercise. I knew it worked now, even when I was distressed, and I appreciated its benefits. My body responded quickly to my breathing, and I cleared my mind with the image of today's snow-covered mountains. I imagined sitting on the log bench, breathing in the fresh mountain air and feeling the sun's warmth on my hands and face, and God's touch.

"Leeta and C.J., become aware of your surroundings and when you're ready, take another deep breath and slowly open your eyes."

I opened my eyes slowly. I was relaxed and ready to begin. Leeta's red patches were gone, and her eyes were soft.

"Okay, C.J., you're the speaker still."

"Leeta, I did enjoy the ride and being with you and Travis. Yes, riding in the cold wet snow is not my thing, but it's yours; therefore, I didn't object because I love you and I wanted, using your words, to be a good sport about it. But I do need time to do things I enjoy too, and making contact on the ham radio is one of them. I would also like some *us* time—that is you and me once and awhile."

"What do you mean?" Leeta asked.

"Not yet, Leeta. What did you understand C.J. to say first?" Jane interrupted.

Leeta took a deep breath. "I understood C.J. to say he enjoyed the ride with Travis and me. Riding in the snow was not his thing but mine. He didn't object because he loved me, and he was being a good sport about it. He needs time to himself and making contact on the radio is one of them. He would like some 'us' time."

"Is that correct?" Jane asked, directing her attention to me.

"Yes."

"Your question?" Jane asked looking at Leeta.

"What kind of 'us' time do you want?"

"Some time with just us," I responded.

"What is that?" Leeta looked directly into my eyes.

"Something like what we did when we were dating." *What I want to scream out is sex. I'm sex deprived!*

Leeta was silent. Jane was quiet. I folded my arms, looked straight ahead and breathed. I was determined there would be no pounding of my heart in my ears or sweating.

Leeta finally broke the silence, ". . . and sex."

"Yes. What happened? When we dated, we were having sex like bunnies in heat. Then we got married and almost nothing."

"You stopped being my boyfriend."

"Huh?"

"You stopped being my boyfriend. You stopped looking at me. When we were dating, you used to be so open with your feelings toward me. You were always surprising me. Like the time you knocked on my front door dressed up as Cupid on Valentine's Day. Or, the time you went out and brought me a CD of my favorite songs and had it playing when you picked me up at work. Do you remember?"

I said nothing, but yes, I remembered.

"You made an effort. We talked all the time. I could say anything to you, and you accepted me for who I was, without criticism. Then when we got married. I lost my boyfriend and my best friend."

Chapter Fifteen

A Second Chance to Get It Right

I CAME TO THE PLANT EARLIER THAN USUAL. MY NIGHT HAD BEEN LONG and sleepless as I tediously watched every passing hour from the yellow glow of our bedside digital clock. I would've loved to have made contact on the radio. It would've been a good distraction from yesterday's session. I feared Leeta would have viewed it as my leaving the marital bed. My mind kept racing with Leeta's words, detailing my attentiveness when we were dating, along with my unconditional acceptance and openness toward her. Then once we got married, she felt she lost her boyfriend and best friend.

"Donuts from McFarlan," Kate said from outside my office door. "We have good news to celebrate."

"We do?" I heard a surprised Robert ask.

"Sure do. Let me get my coat off and start the coffee," Kate answered.

"Wow, you brought a box full." Robert laughed.

"Robert, have you read the paper today?" David queried outside my door.

"No, but it must be good. We're having a party," Robert stated.

Good news was just what my mind and body needed, and to top it off with coffee and a doughnut made it even better. I got up from my desk and headed for the door. Kate had not brought doughnuts in since before Thanksgiving. My mouth started watering, thinking of one of McFarlan's doughnuts slathered with its legendary chocolate frosting.

"Hello," Kate cheerfully said as I opened my door. "Come and join the celebration," she said, showing me *Times-News* front page headlines:

LAWMAKERS PITCH PUBLIC REFERENDUM.

"Huh?"

"Our senator and congresswoman have heard the townfolks' cries about not wanting tall buildings in downtown Hendersonville."

"I still don't understand."

"They slapped an amendment onto another bill out of Kure Beach, North Carolina. This small coastal town is as overwhelmed as we are about runaway new development and high-rises. The amendment allows for a referendum at the January primary on whether the people of Hendersonville want their downtown buildings to be taller than their present sixty-four feet."

"Can the legislature do that?"

"I don't know, but our state representatives are going to try." She read, "Senator Tom says, 'Here's the bottom line, I trust the people of Hendersonville to make this decision.'" Kate looked up from her reading, "You know what that means?"

"Yes. The referendum could nullify the City Council's 3-2 vote in support of taller buildings."

"Yes." David chuckled, pouring himself a cup of Kate's freshly brewed coffee, then biting into a Boston Crème doughnut.

"Knowing you, Kate, you're right in the thick of it." I smiled as I poured myself a hot cup of Joe and reached for my favorite doughnut.

"You know me well, C.J." Kate said proudly.

"You know, you've done more for Hendersonville than I've been able to do on the city planning board. I'm all ears, so tell me what you did."

"I don't know about that. The odds have been stacked against you, because you weren't a part of the 'good old boys' club' on City Council. That will change at the next city election, guaranteed."

"We'll see. I'm still waiting to hear what you did."

Kate extended her left arm to Robert and David, "I, along with them, did nothing differently from any other citizen who was finally fed up with their good-old-boy, self-serving tactics. But from the paper, it appears it has been a lot of us, and Senator Tom says it best." Kate, quoting the senator again from the paper said, 'I can't even go on the streets when I'm home the weekends without being cornered by people, mainly against, saying they're not happy with the process.'" Kate looked up from the paper with a big broad smile. "The referendum was all his idea and Congresswoman Carol's. I didn't have a clue until reading about it in today's paper. But I was one of those people who shared my disappointment with him in town on one of those weekends. You know what he said to me?"

"What?"

Kate walked over to me and looked straight into my eyes, "It's not over until the fat lady sings."

*   *   *

"It's not over until the fat lady sings." You have to love Kate for her tenacity. In the plant's early years, Kate kept the fight in me going by constantly quoting one of Yogi Berra's euphemisms, "It ain't over until it's over."

Kate walking over to me, making direct eye contact and quoting Senator Tom, I knew was a dual message—one for the community and one for me. We're not going to walk away from the fight to preserve the unique character of Hendersonville, and neither are you going to walk away from your marriage. "It's not over until the fat lady sings."

Everybody had left early for the day. I was procrastinating about going home. I tinkered on the new machine. I couldn't have been more pleased with my new invention. It did everything I had hoped for and more. My cell phone rang. It was inside a leather case attached to my belt. I looked at the caller's number. It was Leeta. I was reluctant to answer. "Hello."

"C.J., it's getting late. I wish you would come home, before everything starts freezing over. You know the truck is good in the snow but not on ice."

"I know. Thanks. I'm leaving now."

"I love you."

"Me too."

"Are you okay?"

"Sure. I'll be home directly. Bye."

I wasn't okay, but my saying so to Leeta would force a conversation I wasn't ready to have.

I drove home slowly, being careful to avoid skidding on any black ice. The ride home was peaceful and beautiful. Very few vehicles were out on the roads, and those that were, the drivers drove cautiously. People were decorating earlier this year.

Christmas lights glowed from the houses. Maybe families were making use of the unexpected time off since most businesses were still closed, along with the schools. I turned into the drive leading to the house. As I did, I saw the electric Christmas candles lit in every window, with the front porch light showing off a big Christmas wreath made of boxwood, pinecones and apples on the front door. *Christmas has started here too.* Hannah was standing on the front porch. There was always Hannah, ready to greet me no matter what.

"Hello, girl," I said, leaning down to give her a hug when I got out of the truck. Hannah twirled around in front of me, wagging her tail happily. I walked up to the well-lit kitchen door, decorated with a white pine spray tied with a big red bow. I let both Hannah and myself in. The aroma of homemade goodies penetrated my nostrils. Soft light was coming from two candles sitting on the kitchen table and three more candles grouped together on the kitchen counter. The table was set for two with china and crystal from Leeta's grandmother. I hung my coat up in the mudroom and kicked off my winter boots.

"Hello," Leeta said, walking down from the back kitchen steps and giving me a soft kiss on the mouth when she approached me. Her lavender scent floated gently around her and encircled me. Her hair was not pulled up into a barrette. Instead, her hair hung loosely in soft curls, which touched her shoulders. It shone in the candlelight. She had on a bright red turtleneck, dark slacks and heels. Simple elegance, that's the only word that could describe her.

"Hello," I said, still feeling the sweetness of her kiss on my lips.

"It's just you and me tonight. Travis is spending the night with John. No school tomorrow because the county roads are still so icy."

"Oh." I frankly didn't know what to say. I still was smarting from yesterday's session. "Is this a date?"

A big grin came over Leeta's face. "Yes, I'm asking you on a date."

"A date," I said awkwardly, still being somewhat dumbfounded. How long had it been since we had a date with just us? I couldn't remember one time since we'd been married.

"Yes, 'us time.' You're right it's been a long time since we've had us time and sex like bunnies in heat. I guess I forgot 'the us' in the configuration. I was so focused in making sure Travis wouldn't feel left out, I got the us confused with the family time."

I stood there feeling absolutely numb and speechless. She wasn't adding another egregious wrongdoing to her C.J. shit list. Using Jane Levy's words, Leeta was stating her "participation in the failures with our marriage."

"C.J., what's going on?"

"Umm, I'm shocked."

"Shocked?"

"I wasn't expecting this after yesterday's session."

Leeta laughed. "I'm not surprised."

I sat down at the kitchen table. The candles' flames were straining to be as tall and bright as they possibly could, as if to say, "Don't screw this up, buddy. It takes courage to say I'm sorry."

"I have some wine chilling in the refrigerator." She opened the refrigerator door and got the wine and retrieved a corkscrew from a kitchen drawer. "Will you?" she said as she handed me the wine bottle and corkscrew.

"Sure." I popped the cork and poured the wine into her grandmother's glasses.

"Caesar salad to start our meal, twice-baked potatoes and London broil in the oven. For dessert, Mississippi mud pie with whipped cream."

"All my favorites, thank you."

Leeta lifted up her wine glass and extended it toward me. I did the same, and our glasses touched, making a soft ping. "To us never forgetting *us* ever again," Leeta whispered. "And C.J., I've always loved you and always will, forever and a day."

"Always?" I asked incredulously. I had heard almost those exact words from Cullen, except Leeta was telling me she had *always* loved me.

"Yes, from the first time I saw you at the New Year's party almost eight years ago. My heart did flip flops with our brief encounter at the party. Because I was with a date, it was not the time or the place. You and I didn't even exchange names, but I knew we would meet again.

Wherever I went after our first encounter, I looked for you. When we met outside of Narnia's Studios on Main Street, I was delighted but not surprised. We talked for hours, drinking coffee at the café. The conversation flowed. Remember?"

I nodded. Yes, I remembered and it saddened me how we had grown so far apart.

Leeta continued, "I felt I had known you my entire life. I called my mother afterward, and I told her, 'I've met the man I'm going to marry.'"

I was completely astonished. How many times had I told her it was love at first sight when I saw her across the crowded room at the New Year's Eve party? "You never have told me this."

"No, and I should've, and for that I'm sorry." Leeta turned her face slightly away from me.

I gently turned her face toward me, leaned over and gave her a long slow kiss. "I needed to hear that, thank you." *If she only knew the power she has over me.* At that moment, a light feathery touch brushed across my cheek. *Yes, God, I hear you loud and clear. You're letting me know I've had this opportunity before with Cullen. You're giving me a second chance to get it right this time. I just need to show up and be there.*

* * *

The morning sunlight pierced my eyes and forced them open. *Dear God, what time can it be?* Nine o'clock. I haven't slept this late in years. There was no sign of Leeta, and the house was eerily quiet. All the shutters were open. From the bed, I could see the snow-covered tree limbs glistening like tiny golden jewels. Leeta and I had made love into the wee hours of the morning. Never had I remembered love-making being so spectacular. I sat up, and as I did, I spied an envelope addressed to me in Leeta's handwriting. I reached for it and held it gingerly with both my hands, before sliding my finger slowly underneath the flap on its underside. As I opened the white sheet of folded paper, which had been held captive inside the envelope, my eyes fell upon Leeta's beautiful script that flowed effortlessly across its page:

My darling,

Remember how the night crept in on us.
How its black mist filled the air so nicely,
Wrapped its tail around us,
Whispered into our ears,
Placed its hands on our mouths to hush us.
Did you understand what it said?
Listen . . . carefully.
Let it possess your mind, for you see,
It possesses me.
Leeta

I drew in a deep breath and closed my eyes. Oh yes, Leeta, it possesses me. I pray this time we don't let it go. I opened the drawer of the bedside table, retrieved a pen and a pad of paper . . .

* * *

"Travis, you want to tune the band on the ham radio to see if we can find somebody calling?

"C.Q.," I coached.

"What does C.Q. mean?"

"The letters CQ stand for 'seeking you.' They mean the sender is looking to talk to anybody."

"Sure."

"Turn this knob here. Turn it slowly so you don't miss the call."

"Stop. There is someone calling CQ. Listen to the rhythm dah dit dah dit and dah dah dit dah. Hey, it's an old friend, Mac over in Tennessee. Last time I chatted with him, he was having some trouble with his old tube transmitter. Let's give him a call."

I pounded out his call on my key followed by my call and waited. "Yep. He is coming back to me. See how high the meter bounces? That means he has a strong signal." As I sent the code, I translated to Travis what we were saying to each other. Mac and I did our usual ham chatter about the weather; then I asked him about his transmitter. He said he had to replace a tube, and it took him a few days to find one.

"C.J., what is a tube?" Travis asked somewhat meekly after the signing off.

"Tubes are what 1950s and '60's radios and before used instead of transistors and integrated circuits, which we use today in radios. Tubes have a filament in them that glows like a light bulb. They also have other metal elements in them that catch the electrons given off by the filament."

"Why would anybody want to use such primitive equipment?"

"Well, for the fun of it. The old tube radios actually sound better than the new stuff. Too much digital manipulation goes on now. You interested in getting into ham radio? They recently dropped the requirement to learn Morse code to operate."

"Nah. It's fun hearing about you talking to somebody in New Zealand or some such place, but it sounds like it takes too much luck and patience. If I want to talk to somebody, I'll just text or call them on my cell, and the reception is always good."

"Are you sure I can't interest you in getting into ham radio? It would be a good excuse to get some more equipment and put up another antenna or two."

Travis, looking over at his mother, who had been sitting quietly across the room, smiled. "Sorry. Can't help you there, amigo," he said to me. "You will have to convince Mom some other way to let you buy more toys."

Leeta, sitting in the corner with her reading glasses atop her nose and a book in her hands, laughed aloud.

I handed Travis an envelope. "Then give this to your mother."

"Sure thing," Travis said as he got up, handed his mother the envelope and sat back down in his chair.

Leeta smiled at me as she opened the envelope. She adjusted her reading glasses on the bridge of her nose and read the words aloud:

> It's like a dream,
>   a dream come true;
> A feeling, a need I thought
>   would always be hungry, unfed;
> An answer, a realization that I thought
>   could only come true in sweet sleep.
> I did not know, how could I know,
>   that one so whole existed.
> I only hope she exists for me,
>   and will always be mine.
> If so, meet the happiest
>   man alive today.
> If not, meet the empty
>   carcass of death.
> To you I owe so much
>   and can give so little, but I will try.
> How inadequate.
>
>   88 (love and kisses), C.J.

"Oh, C.J.," Leeta said quietly.

"That will work, C.J." Travis smiled. "More letters like that, I'm sure Mom will let you have the forty-foot tower you keep threatening to get."

Both Leeta and I burst into laughter. *Yeah, this is what it is all about.* I looked at Travis perched on a chair at my arm and his mother, my wife, sitting close by. *You can be sure, God, I'll get it right this time.*

Chapter Sixteen
A Different Leg of Our Journey

"GOOD AFTERNOON." JANE CAME SMILING INTO THE COUNSELING room. "Already seated and ready to work."

"Yes, we sure are," Leeta said. "The door was open, and we just came in and took our places."

"Not quite. I see you're sitting in each other's chairs."

Leeta laughed. "We wondered if you'd noticed. We're on a different leg of our journey together."

Jane sat down in her chair across from ours and picked up her yellow legal pad from the table that sat in between us. "Tell me more."

Leeta continued without skipping a beat, "We took 'us time,' had sex like bunnies in heat, and C.J. got rest from it all with his ham radio and plant time."

Jane began jotting down some notes on her yellow pad. "What changed?"

"I made a decision to stop being angry and made a renewed commitment to C.J."

"You hadn't chosen to work with your anger and commitment to C.J. in our earlier sessions together?"

"Well, I thought I had, but I guess I really hadn't."

Jane looked up from her note taking. "So what changed?"

"I don't know. I just did."

"Nope, I'm not letting you off that easy. What changed?" Jane insisted.

Yeah, what changed? I wondered to myself. *No doubt, it's been a great few days but what did change, and is this going to keep up?*

Leeta moved her lips sideways and then scrunched them together, as she did sometimes when she was in serious thought. "Well, I took time out to breathe deeply and exhale slowly after the last session. I must say the breathing does wonders in getting the bad feelings out of my body, and me back in front brain. Then I was really able to understand what C.J. said in the last session. He was right. He hasn't been on the ham radio in weeks, and we haven't had 'us time' since I don't know when. I was able to give him credit for that mostly. He has been attentive since we started counseling. He's asked me on several occasions what he could do to help, and both Travis and C.J. have been good about picking up what they mess up. But I guess I was fearful when it all might stop. I was afraid to let my guard down, so I picked at every little something that wasn't exactly as I thought it should be."

Jane looked down at her notes and read, "Breathe deeply and exhale slowly, get the bad feelings out of your body, return to your front brain, choose not to be angry, and recommit to us. Leeta, did I understand you correctly?"

"Perfectly." Leeta's face was luminous. It had been a long time since I'd seen her so radiant.

"So you've chosen a new pattern to work out your distress and conflicts?" Jane questioned.

"I haven't thought of it that way," Leeta said, "but yes that's what I did."

"Empowered?" Jane interjected.

"Well, yes, that too," Leeta said slowly. She turned and looked at me.

I didn't know what to say. I was pleased with Leeta's affirmations, but cautious too. We've been here before, stating our recommitment and make-up sex. The only differences within the past year, more often than not, are that those periods were replaced with louder and meaner arguments.

"C.J.," Jane stated.

Now it was my turn. *Breathe deeply, exhale slowly,* repeating to myself Leeta's phrase. The rhythm of the phrase was in keeping for a deep relaxed breath. "What?"

"Are you on a new leg of your journey with Leeta?"

"Well, hopefully. We definitely had a great weekend for sure, plenty of 'us time.' I did enjoy being on the ham radio, mainly because Leeta was okay with me doing so. Both Leeta and Travis enjoyed hearing about some of my contacts to different parts of the country and the world."

"What changed?"

What changed? I don't know, I thought to myself. However, I clearly understood the "I don't know" answer wasn't going to work with Jane. "Leeta changed. She apologized and planned a lovely evening and next day for us. She said she understood what I was saying about us not having time together."

"So it was Leeta who changed?"

"Yes."

"You didn't?"

I readjusted myself in my chair. I took another deep breath to better mull over what else I needed to say. *She'd called for me to come home early. When I got home, she had changed her attitude toward me. She changed. That's it.* "I don't know what else you're wanting me to say."

"Well, what I understood you to say so far was you were hopeful you were on a different leg of your journey with Leeta. And what changed was Leeta. Was that correct?"

"Yes, that's correct."

"You didn't participate at all in the success of the date you two had together?"

Oh yeah, I reflected, remembering one of Jane's major points in our early sessions, *"It takes two to do the dance." We both participated in the failures of our marriage. It'll take two to participate in its successes.* "I can't think of anything I did, except show up and be there."

"Bingo. There would be no way Leeta's date with you could have been successful without your allowing it."

"Yes, that true."

"How come you allowed it to happen?"

"Because I love her, and I want our relationship to work. But, I guess I'm skeptical because Leeta and I have been at this place before—wonderful weeks, or months together, and then it falls apart. The only consistent good times we've had together were when we were dating." Jane hadn't taken her eyes off me. *What does she want from me? What's the right answer? If I didn't know better, I would think she was reading my every thought—a* Twilight Zone *TV Land moment, complete in black and white.*

Jane stated carefully, "This is my hallucination only. Instead of you spending an inordinate amount of time on the ham radio, long hours at work or tinkering with a car that really needs no tinkering and thereby limiting your time with Leeta, you're now choosing to breathe deeply and exhale slowly, get the bad feelings out of your body and stay in the front brain, so you can allow yourself to show up and be there with Leeta."

My mouth flew up. "What you've just listed are all of the things I really enjoy doing."

"Stay with me, C.J. I made neither statement nor inference to you not enjoying them. What did I say?"

"About your hallucination?"

"Yes, just a theory about what's changed within you and toward this relationship with Leeta."

"Your theory is that I'm choosing to breathe deeply, exhale slowly, get the bad feelings out of my body, stay in the front brain, so I can allow myself to show up and be there with Leeta. Instead of choosing not to be with Leeta by staying long hours at the plant, doing unnecessary work on the Volvo or spending an inordinate amount of time on the ham radio?"

"Yep, that's my hallucination. Is that correct?"

"Almost."

"Really?" Leeta gasped. "You did all of those things to stay away from me?"

I looked over at Leeta, the light dim in her eyes, and I quickly added, "Well, I didn't realize it until Jane asked me if her 'hallucination' about me was true. When you called me last week to come home before everything started to freeze over again, I was procrastinating about coming home."

"C.J., you said almost," Jane stated.

"Yes, your theory is correct. But there is more."

"What?" Jane asked.

"I am changing. I know the breathing is helping me feel better. I don't feel I'm going to have a heart attack anymore. I'm stepping back more with things that used to give me a knee-jerk reaction, like being behind someone who is driving below the speed limit or being stuck in traffic on I-26. So yes, I'm changing too and because of these changes, I was able to show up and be there that night and the next for you, Leeta. And for me, I loved every minute of it." I looked at Leeta again and saw a smile on her face and the light back in her eyes. Leeta's eyes filled with tears as she mouthed, thank you. "And one other thing, God is helping me get it right this time."

Jane nodded and smiled assuredly. "When one learns how to quiet his or her mind with breathing or meditation exercises, it is not unusual that the heart and mind open to God's wisdom and His peace. Prayer and deep breathing can be interchangeable."

"I agree, but I think God has been talking to me all along. I've just been able to really hear him in the past couple of weeks."

Jane nodded her head again. "So C.J. and Leeta, because you're appreciating the fact, it takes two to do the dance and the added benefit of knowing God is giving you a helping hand, you have developed a very solid foundation to do the marriage success dance together."

"What are the steps?" Leeta asked.

"The steps, you two make up. The dance is choreographed by both of you, creating the balance and mutually agreed upon 'rights,' which two people need to live together 'till death do us part.'"

"I'm ready to choreograph the dance with you, C.J.," Leeta said as she squeezed my hand. "There's no way we cannot make a beautiful dance together with God walking beside us."

Jane smiled. "Let's go over what you've learned so far in our work together. You married for the right reasons—you love each other, have fun together, have a lot in common, and have just enough difference to learn from. You've learned that every intimate relationship has inherent living issues. You've both participated in your marriage disappointments as well as its successes.

"And blaming is off the table because it is a technique to get you off the hook to do anything differently than what you were already doing. The focus is on your participation, the only area you have power over. Not what your partner does. You've been managing your anger with breathing exercises to stay in the front brain and practicing listening skills. Understanding that right and wrong is a relative concept, which is defined by the individual or the couple. If it works, it's right; and if doesn't work, it's wrong. Finally, the goal of stopping the 'loud mean arguments with no resolutions' is not to win the argument but to negotiate a mutually agreed upon right. You've already begun the process of negotiating two of them—time together/time apart and home maintenance."

I was amazed. In less than a minute, she summarized all our work together. "How many sessions have we had with you, six?" I asked.

Jane put on her reading glasses as she reached for a white card on the side table. "Seven, why?"

"You've summarized all the major points of our seven sessions in less than a minute . . ." I struggled to find the words to express what I really wanted to say. Jane smiled, encouraging me to continue. "None of this has been easy for me, but the points you've identified in our work together, now seem so obvious, just common sense."

"You've made a paradigm shift in your thinking."

"Yes, I guess I have."

"And it feels what?"

"Good, very good. Better tools than what I did have. Now things that seemed so impossible to work on before, do not now."

"Excellent, because you two still have two more issues to work on."

"What's that?" Leeta and I asked in unison.

"Money and sex."

Chapter Seventeen
Robert's Deliberation

"**I**t works like a charm," said Robert as he rubbed down the machine from top to bottom. "I didn't think you could improve on what we already had, but by golly you did."

"Yeah, I'm pleased, but I couldn't have done it without your assistance."

"Hello, fellas." Kate waved as she walked hurriedly past us, humming, "It's Beginning to Look a Lot Like Christmas."

"Boy, she's been more chipper than usual during the holiday season," I stated to Robert. If anybody got into the holiday spirit, it was Kate. This year she had gone way out, by including employees' families in decorating the smaller white pines on the plant's hundred-acre woods with the edible decorations.

"A *Hendersonville Lightning* reporter is coming today to do a feature story on the white pine, edible, tree decorations for Wednesday's paper," Robert informed me.

"When did this all come about?"

"Yesterday. You had already left for the day."

"Yes, Leeta and I had our Tuesday-at-four appointment with Jane Levy."

"You're still going?"

"Yes, we're still going. Yesterday was our seventh session."

Robert abruptly finished rubbing down the machine and stuffed the rag in his back pocket. He had stopped smiling, making his angular good looks even more austere. "How is it?"

I didn't answer immediately. His question wasn't just for curiosity's sake. He was dating his ex-wife. "Well, it's probably the hardest thing I've ever done, but at the same time, the most rewarding." I paused to collect my thoughts. We both, being engineers, understood words didn't flow as rapidly as drawings did in expressing our ideas. "Therapy offers us a safe environment to state our complaints with each other. We're learning how to manage our anger to stop the loud, mean arguments we were having. Jane Levy has given us tools for communicating, and she coaches us in using them effectively. There are no bad guys or good guys. We're both participators in the failures and successes in our marriage. And best of all, we're a normal couple working with normal living issues." I beamed with my articulation of what we'd learned in counseling.

Robert's austere look didn't change as he slowly stated, "So you highly recommend couple's counseling."

"I guess I am, and I'm not embarrassed to say I'm in marriage counseling with Leeta."

"Hmm." Robert pushed his hair away from his forehead as he always did. Of course, his cowlick made sure that his sandy blond hair didn't stay put but fell disobediently back onto his forehead. "So this Jane Levy you think is good?"

"For us, she is."

"What do you mean?"

"She'll tell you that in the first session. The first step in counseling is to make sure everyone feels comfortable with each other. I believe those were her exact words."

"What's it like being in counseling?"

"Well." I paused again to come up with the perfect words to describe my experience. "What's it like? It's like talking with your best friend, but different too. When your best friend asks how you're doing and you say fine, that's the end of it. But when your therapist asks you how you're doing and you say fine, she'll ask, 'What do you mean?'"

"No short answers, huh?"

I laughed. "No short answers."

Chapter Eighteen
"Why Don't You Trust Me?"

"So this Kate Burton is a long time employee of yours?" Jane asked, sitting down in her usual chair.

"Yes. She was the first person I hired and has been with me now close to sixteen years. She informed me on her sixty-fifth birthday she had no plans to retire any time soon."

"Good write up about her and your plant doing good things for the wildlife in the *Hendersonville Lightning*," Jane said.

"All her idea, and the holiday spirit of giving and doing goodwill for all creatures has really boosted the employees' morale, like I never witnessed before."

"Good for her. From the write-up, she's involved in every possible way to preserve the history and the natural character of the area, becoming involved with the Preservation Society, Downtown Alliance and Western North Carolina Land Conservancy."

"I'm finding that out day by day," I said.

"You say that with some reservation . . ."

"Well, you can't say no to Kate," I said, looking over at Leeta.

Leeta laughed. "I like to say she's infectious with her causes. What I think C.J. is referring to is Kate gets everybody involved with her good intentions. Whether we want to or not. We're now decorating our small trees with edible decorations on *our* property, and she has encouraged every employee to do the same on theirs."

"Again, good for her." Jane laughed. "It was a great feel-good story. My family now is discussing how we can best help the displaced wildlife in a responsible manner. But enough chit-chat, how are you doing?"

"Fine," we both responded.

"And what does that mean?"

I gave a fervent laugh, remembering what I said to Robert about my experience being in counseling.

Jane smiled, looking curiously at me. "Yes?"

"I have a friend who was quizzing me about being in marriage counseling."

"Yes."

"Well, I said it was like talking to your best friend. Except the difference being, when your best friend asks how you're doing and you say fine, that's the end of it. But when your counselor asks how you're doing and you say fine, she'll ask, 'what do you mean?'"

"Thank you, and another gem for my treasure chest. How was your week?"

Leeta answered first, "It's been good. We're having more 'us time,' but not forgetting the family time. I've been very busy getting ready for the holidays. I do a lot of holiday gift baking, and this year, I've been especially busy making edible tree decorations for the plant and home. Travis and I have been riding the horses on the plant's property with our satchel of goodies. C.J. rode with us on Sunday. We've never done this before. It's been good."

"I agree," I said. "I think we're finding a balance between our together and apart time."

I didn't mention my still not getting enough sex time. It was indeed better for sure, but not like it was when we were dating.

"Good for you," Jane responded. "We still have two issues we haven't worked with, sex and money."

Sounds like a movie title, I reflected.

"Leeta, if memory serves me correctly, your issue was being off balance with the money, and C.J., you're feeling off balance with the sex. You've have the skills now to process them out and negotiate a solution that works for both of you. Who wants to begin?"

Not me, I mused.

"I will, I guess," Leeta said. "It's way past time we've talked about money."

"Okay then," Jane said. "So, Leeta, you're the speaker. C.J., you're the listener. Don't forget your stop tools, since you're responsible for all of Leeta's information and to understand it *exactly* as she wants you to understand it."

I nodded.

Leeta turned and faced me directly. "C.J., I feel you don't trust me. There's nothing in my name, except for the house. The truck isn't in my name, but you say it's my truck. You have your checking and savings account, and I have mine. You say you have a life insurance policy with my being the beneficiary, but I've never seen it. We have no Will together, even though you say we do need one, but somehow you never have the time to make an appointment with an attorney. You did manage to hire a lawyer to write up a prenuptial before we were married, to prevent me from attaching any claim on Commercial International Insulations' assets in case of a divorce. You've made sure each and every one of your employees will be well taken care of upon their retirement or your death, but not Travis or me."

I was quiet and calm.

"C.J., what did you understand Leeta to say?"

"In a nutshell, she feels I don't trust her and gave a litany of examples to make her point."

Jane turned to Leeta, "Any comments?"

"Well, yes, those are a list of examples to make my point on why I feel, C.J., you don't trust me, but that list also says how many ways you haven't really included me or Travis in your life."

She's right, I thought. *But what is impressing me the most is the nonplussed feeling I am having. I feel almost dead inside.*

"C.J., your thoughts?" Leeta asked.

My thoughts . . . so what do I say now. Do I talk about my nonplussed feelings, or my feeling dead inside? "You're correct," I finally said. "There's nothing in our name except for the house. Everything else is in my name. There is no Will, but there is a prenuptial. There is a life insurance policy, and you're the beneficiary. No, you've never seen it. I understand why you feel I don't trust you and why you feel I haven't included you or Travis in my life. Did I understand you *exactly* as you want me to understand you?" I asked condescendingly. I looked directly into Leeta's very dark sad eyes. I watched them fill slowly with tears, trickling one after another down her cheeks onto her very full lips and off her chin.

I didn't know how much time passed, nor did I care before Jane finally spoke, "C.J., what's going on with you."

"I don't know."

"You don't know?"

"No, I don't know." I heard Leeta sniffling, and the table clock ticking loudly on the side table. Odd, I haven't heard its ticktock since our earlier sessions together. But I wasn't sweating, nor did I hear my heart beat in my ears.

"C.J., please hand Leeta a Kleenex," Jane encouraged.

"Sure," I heard myself say. I was feeling more hollow inside and distant. As I handed Leeta the Kleenex box, I saw her pink cheeks being soaked with her tears, and her nostrils emitting a clear liquid. I didn't have a flicker of concern for my distressed wife. In fact, if anything, I felt rising a feeling of antipathy.

"C.J., what's going on?" Jane coaxed.

"I don't know," I said in an irritated tone.

"You don't know," Jane said quietly. "Okay then, it does appear you understand what Leeta said, but do you agree?"

"No."

"Why?" asked Jane.

"Why that should be obvious." I was becoming increasingly annoyed.

"Apparently not," Jane replied.

"God, what do you want from me, Leeta?" I retorted acidly. "Hasn't life improved for you immensely since you've been married to me? You're now able to do what you've always wanted to do—build a business as a horse trainer and be a stay-at-home mom. You weren't financially able to do either before marrying me. You were doing a nine-to-five job you detested and able to ride only on the weekends, if that much. Now you own three horses, instead of one. When will enough be enough for you? What do I have to do or be to satisfy you?"

"Who are you talking about, C.J.? It certainly isn't me," Leeta asserted. She was no longer crying, but her face was still flushed. "I've heard these accusations before. Number one, I was happy in my job. I found my job challenging. I was paying the bills and providing a home for Travis and me. Yes, I owned one horse, but Mr. Collis leased me Sheba at a price I could afford, which was simply to take care of her. I've heard your description more than once about the scraggily ass fence and the decrepit shed I kept the horses in. What are you saying about me? My life was dismal, until my knight in shining armor on his handsome white steed rode into my life, scooping us up into his strong arms and riding off into the sunset to live happily ever after?"

"Huh." *What a jolt. She's right. One of the things that attracted me to her was her self-confident independence and that she took care of her son and herself well and lovingly.* I now remembered her saying, "I come packaged, my son and I come together. I don't need anybody to take care of me. What I want is somebody to care about me and me him. Somebody I love being with and he with me. But, I need you to take care of my son along with me and include him in our life together. I don't do this living together stuff, but marriage is not a dress rehearsal either. It is a commitment, 'till death do us part.'"

Leeta's face was no longer flushed. In fact, she possessed an uncanny calm. "C.J., who are you talking about? I don't even recognize this person who you accuse me of on a regular basis when we're fighting. I now understand what you believe about me, I can't change. I'm tired of fighting this phantom, and I won't stay in a marriage in which I'm constantly defending me."

"What's that old Chinese saying, 'Be careful what you wish for, you might get it'? Is that an ultimatum?" I asked tersely.

"If that's what you want to call it, yes."

The table clock's ticking became louder and louder, as I sat stone-faced and quiet. Finally, I stated, "I'm in this marriage all the way to the finish line."

"Nope, not that easy a fix. Who is this person I get accused of being constantly?"

"I don't know, but you're right, she's not you."

"Not good enough. At least, you've identified this person as a she. Until you identify her, I'll always be confused with her. Figure it out."

Figure it out. Leeta's words were playing and replaying in my head.

A proliferation of feelings came rushing into my emptiness—sadness, anger, loss, hurt, betrayal, loneliness. Then I heard an animal-like cry roaring from within me. It took me over and nothing I could do to stop it. I felt this gentle hand being placed on my knee, and saw soulful dark eyes looking up at me; then two loving arms wrapped around my shaking shoulders. "Who is she?" Leeta asked.

"My mother."

* * *

"Are you okay?" Leeta asked, as I backed the car out of the parking space and drove the car forward.

"Not really."

"Do you want to talk?"

"Not now, Leeta."

"Okay, but please, C.J., DON'T SHUT ME OUT. WHAT AFFECTS YOU, AFFECTS ME TOO."

I stopped the car abruptly at the end of Jane Levy's office driveway before exiting out onto Sixth. I'd heard those exact words from Cullen. I turned, looked over at Leeta and feigned a smile.

* * *

I did my best at dinner to appear normal, and that was far from how I felt. Travis made dinner talk easy as always with his daily stories about his classmates and teachers. The kid was funny, unlike me when I was his age. After dinner, I helped Leeta with the dishes. I even asked if I could help with the night feeding of the horses and getting them blanketed.

"No, C.J., I'm good. How about popcorn and wine later in front of the fire."

"Sounds good," I said, heading toward the den. I took some newspaper from Leeta's grandmother's coal bin, crumbled it up and laid it on the fireplace grate. I took kindling from the bucket beside the fireplace and placed several pieces, teepee style on top of the crumpled paper, then carefully laid the logs of hardwood on top. I took a long matchstick from a brass container on the mantle and lit the newspaper. I sat down on the couch and watched the fire slowly ignite itself—first the newspaper, then the kindling and finally the firewood. I could feel myself breathe easily as I watched the flames dance before me. They lulled me into a trance. Cullen's and now Leeta's plea not to shut her out became the unrelenting thought etching itself deep into my brain.

I never knew if my mother loved me. I have no memory of her ever telling me so. I do remember vividly her having a tongue like a double-edged sword. I learned early how to shut her out to avoid being stabbed by it. As the years went by, I saw my father do the same by staying longer and longer hours at work. My sister did not. She challenged my mother any way she could.

When my mother left my father, he said it was best I lived with Mother. I understood why. He had become a beaten-down man with my mother's never-ending complaints of him not doing enough or making enough money. He didn't need to deal with another added complaint of him not being a good enough father. After eight years of an ugly and raucous marital property dispute, he then became an embittered old sick man. He died a few years later.

Marital property dispute, I repeated the phrase in my head. *If I changed the I and T in the word marital to T and I, it would spell martial.* I walked over to the bookshelf and retrieved *The Merriam-Webster Dictionary.* I thumbed through the pages until I found the M words. Then I ran my finger down the page until I found martial. Words used to define it were armed, carrying weapons, fortified. Then I ran my finger up the page and found marital. Words used to define it were wedded, conjugal, matrimonial, connubial. Interesting, how close the two words are in its spelling, and just by switching side by side letters, how different they were in meaning. In the case of my parents, their relationship was more warlike than matrimonial. I returned the dictionary to its place on the bookshelf. I stoked the fire with the poker, and with each jab, the flames grew higher and crackled louder. I returned to my place on the couch and watched the flames become calmer and quieter.

I closed my eyes and memories of Cullen's and our "martial" relationship raced through my memory tract as if I were fast-forwarding a DVD. The memory DVD stopped at the scenes where Cullen was constantly hurt by my mother's condescending arrogance. Many of our fights centered on my not standing up to Mother in Cullen's behalf. I told Cullen it would make matters only worse for her and me if I did. There was no way I could convince Cullen. Cullen always viewed my resistance to confront my mother as my being spineless and betraying her, that my love for my mother came before her.

Dear God, I'm weary with all this. I've always prided myself in being able to compartmentalize my feelings. This set of memories I thought I had locked away and purposely lost the key. Apparently not. My head pounded and sharp dagger-like pain pierced my eyes.

"C.J," Leeta said quietly as she sat down beside me. She was holding a tray, which held two hot steaming mugs and a big, wooden bowl of popcorn. "Are you all right?"

"Not really."

"Do you want to talk about it?"

"No, Leeta. I just need to sort this out by myself." I picked up one of the mugs, lifted it to my nose and felt the heat from the steam soothe my aching head. "I know this isn't wine."

"Aunt Dollie's hot buttered rum. It has milk in it with a touch of nutmeg. She and my uncle had them every night in the winter before they went to bed. She would say, 'It's the grown-up version of drinking warm milk to help you go to sleep.'"

I took a sip and felt its soothing, warm liquid trickle down my throat. "Delicious, thank you."

Leeta sat the tray on the table beside the couch and picked up her drink and the bowl of popcorn. She set the popcorn between us. She leaned back onto the couch, brought her legs up and crossed them Indian style. We sat together, drinking our hot toddies, slowly munching on the popcorn until we grew full.

"C.J., I'm going to bed," Leeta whispered, standing up and placing the empty wooden bowl and mugs on the tray. "Come with me?"

"Later. I'll be up later," I said barely above a whisper.

"Don't be too long, please."

I nodded. I don't know how long I sat there staring at the flames, but it had to be into the wee hours of the morning. I quietly went up the stairs to our bedroom, stripped my clothes off and let them drop on the floor beside the bed. I had only enough energy to go to the bathroom to pee and crawl into the bed. Leeta folded perfectly into me. I wrapped my top arm around her waist and pulled her closer, until my lips brushed across her silken hair and her sweet lavender scent filled up my senses. "Thy will be done. I'll leave this in your hands, Lord," I whispered. I felt a soft, feathery touch brush across my cheek. I closed my eyes and fell into a deep peaceful sleep with my Leeta close to my heart.

*　*　*

The harsh shrill of the telephone ring abruptly propelled me out of bed. I felt nausea from the unexpected, cruel jolt. I stood by the bed, rubbing my chest feverishly, trying to orient myself. The phone rang again and seemingly an octave louder and even more jarring than before. The invasion of sunlight from the open shutters burned into my eyes. Leeta was not in the bed nor Hannah in hers. The phone rang again.

"Hel-hello," I stuttered in a gravelly low voice.

"C.J., did I wake you?" Kate's voice loomed out of the telephone.

"Yes," I muttered. I saw black and quickly lay back down on the bed before I passed out.

"What? Are you okay?" Kate asked hesitantly.

"I don't know."

"You don't know?"

"Maybe I am okay."

"Well, are you or are you not? Leeta is here with Ajax riding in the woods. She came with treats over an hour ago. Do I need to have Robert or David find her and tell her to go home?"

"No, I'm okay. The phone ringing had catapulted me out of a very sound sleep. I'd never slept so deeply, nor been awakened so abruptly. I'm just trying to get my ground legs."

Kate was silent.

I finally said, "Kate, are you there?"

"Yes." She remained silent. I knew Kate well enough to know she was worried about me, but Kate being Kate was carefully deciding exactly how she should proceed. "C.J., are you planning to come in today?"

Yep, that was Kate, never pushy. Tenacious, resolute, yes. "Hmm, I don't know. I'll call you within the hour if I decide not to come in."

"Please do. Goodbye."

I lay in bed looking up at the ceiling. I watched the sunlight dance merrily across it and found myself becoming less and less nauseated and my body less and less traumatized. I took a deep, slow breath and blew it out with a sigh. Out of the corner of my eye, I saw a white envelope on the bedside table. I rolled over and picked it up from the table. C.J. was written in Leeta's handwriting on the front of the envelope. Sitting up on the edge of the bed, I opened the carefully folded white paper inside and began to read:

My Love Poem

I ask you never to doubt my love,
    or ask the depth or breadth of it
    for I could never explain it in words.
They are only symbols of my love,
    but my eyes express the all of it.
There you can find all the joy and pain
    my love for you does to me
    as it takes its sharp edges
    and lunges for my heart.
You can feel it when my lips touch yours,
    all the tenderness and fire of it.
No, C.J., I'll never be able to explain
    my love for you in words,
    a feeling that swoops me up so high
    and then,
Suddenly with no reason
    Sends me crashing
        Heart first
            Onto a cement floor
            And there I lie
                Sprawled
                    Reluctant to stand
                    And doubting your love for me,
                        Leeta

Chapter Nineteen
Cracks in My Pillar

JANE EXTENDED HER HAND TOWARD MINE FOR A HANDSHAKE, AND then shook Leeta's. "Thanks for agreeing to see me twice this week, but I felt it necessary after Tuesday's session. And because we won't be having another session until after the New Year."

I nodded as we sat down in our respective chairs.

"How to begin?" Jane asked in her usual relaxing style.

I shrugged my shoulders. I did not want to re-experience the emotional overload of last session or the other night.

"C.J, how to begin?" Jane asked again.

Jane was being her persistent self, and of course Leeta sat beside me coaxing me with her eyes. Then I spoke, "What's the point of this anyway? I haven't seen, spoken, much less thought about the woman in years."

"You mean your mother?" Jane confirmed.

"Yes."

"Point taken, but I saw a man last session who gave the appearance he was in a great deal of emotional distress."

"Yeah, I was surprised with my emotions too," I muttered.

"Excuse me, I didn't hear you."

"I was surprised, too."

"C.J., I see relationships in three entities," Jane announced. "My metaphor to describe this best is a bridge. The bridge is the relationship with its inherent living issues. The two pillars holding up the bridge are the two individuals in the relationship. Most of our work has been directed toward learning how to negotiate balances between you and Leeta with your living issues. But, what is as important as resolving your living issues together is working out the cracks in your individual pillars." Jane stopped but did not make eye contact with either Leeta or me. I've come to expect when she did this, she was carefully contemplating her choice of words to emphasize certain work was to be done— mandatory in fact. This time I clearly understood the onus was on me.

"C.J., if my memory serves me correctly, Leeta felt she was being accused of being someone she wasn't. I think her exact words were that she was tired of fighting the phantom, and that she wasn't going to stay in a marriage in which she was constantly defending herself. Is that what you remember?"

"Yes." I was curt. I really didn't want to talk about my mother, or anything from my childhood, for that matter.

"C.J., you have some cracks in your pillar, and these cracks have and will continue to do damage to your marriage if not dealt with."

"Okay, okay." I took a deep breath and exhaled slowly, hoping to get out the yuck that was rapidly infiltrating my body since the hour began. "The last time I heard from my mother was at Christmas, years ago when my holiday card to her was returned unopened and stamped with 'RETURN TO SENDER, NO SUCH ADDRESSEE.' That was . . ." I paused as I quickly counted the years in my head. ". . . seventeen years ago. That's right, because Cullen and I were still together."

"I don't understand." Jane made direct eye contact with me.

"My mother moved without telling me and left no forwarding address with the postal service."

"I thought you said she lived in Houston."

"I did, but I didn't find out where she moved, until my sister told me a few months later on one of her biannual telephone calls. She found out from her middle son, who has maintained a relationship with his grandmother.

"Biannual telephone calls?"

"Yep. I don't call Peg. She calls me. She doesn't want me to have her telephone number or address because she claims to be in some top-level job, which doesn't allow her to give out any personal information. She states this policy is for her protection as well as mine, and so she calls *me*."

Jane blew out slowly. "How do you feel about all of this?"

"I don't." I answered robotically. "When Mother moved to Houston with her second husband and disinherited me, I thought maybe it was for the best—"

"Disinherited you?" Jane interrupted.

"Well, I can only assume so. She disinherited Peg. A couple of years before she moved to Houston, she sent me her revised Will giving Peg Anne Alfred one penny. Yep, I'm sure I've been disinherited too, along with my childhood pictures taken out of the family album—"

"Excuse me?" Jane interrupted me again.

"From the family albums, my mother cut Peg out of every family picture she was in and removed every picture of just her. Pictures of Peg on tabletops or hanging on walls disappeared too. Poof, one child gone like she never existed." I stopped abruptly. My thoughts hung on to . . . *Poof, one child gone like she never existed. Poof, another child gone like he never existed.*

"What's happening?"

"Nothing."

"That's what I'm afraid of?"

"What do you mean?"

"I don't know exactly. Your whole countenance is changing, even the tone of your voice."

"You notice it too," Leeta blurted out. "I don't even recognize him when he gets like this. It scares me."

Both women were now looking at me. The words, "get me out of here," ran across my brain like the news tape that runs along the bottom of the television screen of Headline News.

"C.J., what are you thinking?" Jane asked with care.

"Leaving."

Jane smiled. "Leave and tinker on a Volvo that really needs no tinkering."

"What?"

"That's what you do when things get prickly, tinker on the Volvo, play on the ham radio or stay at work long hours. Right?"

"Prickly?"

"Yes."

"You know this is something I don't want to do," I retorted. "This is about Leeta and me, not my mother and me."

"Yes, but it's necessary. If you don't process out your relationship with your mother and maybe other family members, Leeta is always going to be defending herself against you with stuff that has nothing do with her."

I rolled my eyes in resignation. For years, my hurt, my confusion, the anger of my childhood had lain dormant. I thought I was over it. I astonished myself when the animal-like cry heaved out of me in Tuesday's session. Once again, every painful memory flashed in front of me like an old eighty's slide projector, projecting every bad picture I ever took. "Prickly is a good word to describe my mother. She had a tongue like a double-edge sword. I had learned early on not to challenge her. One of Cullen's and my countless arguments was my never standing up in Cullen's defense despite my mother's frequent critical remarks toward Cullen. But confronting my mother was pointless. I overheard her say to my father more than once that she didn't lose arguments. My sister, who was six years my senior, never got it. She was eventually beaten down by mother's razor-sharp tongue and cool persona."

"Where was your father during all of this with your mother and older sister?" asked Jane.

"At work mostly."

"You?

A smile crossed my face, "In my room, shooting empty blanks from my .22 rifle into the High Point telephone book, which was strategically placed in my closet."

"Your parents didn't know you were doing that?" Jane asked incredulously.

"I did it when nobody was home. But later my target practice sessions were replaced with my new hobby— ham radio and learning Morse code. I tested out for my ham radio license at the age of twelve," I said proudly.

Words began to spew out of my mouth like lava blown out of the top of an erupting volcano. "When I was twelve, my parents separated and thirteen months after the divorce, both were remarried. My mother insisted that my sister choose between my dad and her. Peg tried hard not to become involved, but instead, old feuds between Mother and her re-ignited Peg's feelings about being replaced, rather than displaced when I was born. Peg became pregnant and married at eighteen and left with her nineteen-year-old husband. I was simply told by my father I was to live with my mother. By then, Mother had beaten Dad down by her constant complaints of him not making enough money to support what she called a 'decent life style.'" He was tired of the fighting. Enough was never enough for her. I've already told you that at fifteen, I moved out of my mother's house because of the relationship I had with my stepfather, and . . . her too, to be honest."

That damn mental projector kept flashing every awful memory of my childhood and my words kept spewing. "Dad had his pilot license. He told me during their separation that he had flown his small plane directly over our house with the full intention of flying the plane directly into it, killing both Mother and him. He said that he would have if he'd known for sure the grandbaby or I weren't in the house. It took eight long years before marital debts and property were settled between them, and by then I was a junior in college. My parents each felt I was spying for the other, because I visited both of them on my brief visits home from school."

Leeta had not uttered a word. She wanted to know about my family. Here it is, the bad and the ugly, and the more ugly. Every bit of it.

Jane sat quietly, jotting down notes on her yellow pad. She reread all her notes and underlined as she read. Then she stated, "Well, there's a lot here, but one thing comes out loud and clear."

"What's that?"

"Your learning as a child, very creative and ingenious ways on how to avoid confrontation and people. Your understanding clearly if your sister couldn't beat your mother in a word fight, you surely couldn't. It appeared your father just stopped trying. He went to work. You immersed yourself into the ham radio and Morse code with the dits and the dahs in the confines of your bedroom. Before that, target practice with the High Point telephone book. And Peg, the consummate avoider, held back on any personal contact information, giving her complete control of when and how she wanted to be with her family."

"I guess so."

"For sure your childhood was difficult."

"For sure," I muttered softly.

"Are you okay?" Jane asked.

"Yeah." Not really, but I didn't want to say I wasn't. "I wasn't proud of my childhood. My sister, when she divorced her husband, did the same thing as my mother did in that she insisted her oldest, her son, choose between the father and her. He chose his dad as Peg did. He got married young and didn't invite my sister to his wedding, then left town not to be heard from ever again. What is so eerie is her son looks exactly like my father when he was a young man. She took her youngest, a daughter, with her as my mother did me, and my niece attempted suicide at fourteen as my sister did when she was fourteen." There was more to tell, but I grew weary with all the painful memories.

"C.J., you're not okay," Jane stated softly.

"No, I'm not okay. But . . ."

"But what?"

"My childhood is what it is, and my talking about it is not helpful."

"Yes, to the degree that your past can't be changed, it is what it is. But frequently, when you allow yourself to tell your story aloud, it helps you understand yourself better, the choices you've already made and the changes you can make. The circumstances of your childhood are your parents' choices, not yours. It has nothing to do with you. Yes, it affected you, but it wasn't because of you."

"What?"

"I'll say it another way. The only way history repeats itself is if you choose it. Whom we choose to marry is frequently one of the ways we choose to change ourselves and our history for the next generation.

"What do you mean?" *Jeez, what does she mean? Again, her words flow nicely together, but to me, just more psychobabble mumbo jumbo.*

"You've heard this before, but I'll add more dimension to what I've already said. You do remember what I said about marrying someone for the right reasons."

"Yes."

"What are they?"

"You're attracted to how she looks; 'beauty is in the eyes of the beholder'; you have fun together, a lot in common and enough difference to learn from."

"Perfect, but then why do one out of two marriages end in divorce?"

"Because they didn't figure out the balance needed to live together." *Jeez, I feel I'm taking a semester exam, enough already.*

"Bear with me, C.J., just a little longer. The hour is almost up."

What is she, psychic? I acquiesced reluctantly. "Okay."

"I'll stop asking questions. I'll just make my points. Negotiating the balance needed to live together happily ever after is easier said than done, as you two have discovered. But why? Because outside of having fun together and having a lot in common, we bring to the marital table our differences. Some of these differences are our values and good intentions. When we present them to each other, and they are challenged as being unimportant, wrong or even stupid, this can be both hurtful and confusing. This is when the first stage of our growing relationship—the honeymoon stage—comes to an end. It is not to say the love stops, but our rose-colored glasses are removed. Frequently, when a couple enters into the second stage of their developing relationship, aptly named the power-struggle stage, they frequently become adversaries instead of negotiators in working out their differences. Their goal is to win instead of negotiating solutions that work for both of them. Unfortunately, this is all too common, and probably the single-most driving force in why fifty percent of our marriages end in divorce. Do you understand what I'm saying?"

"Yes," Leeta said, "like I think beds need to be made every day and Travis and C.J. think why bother. It's just going to be unmade when you go to bed. Or, I'm a firm believer all food should be eaten in the kitchen or at the dining room table. C.J. and Travis say nothing's better when watching a football game on television or a 'kick-ass, blood-spewing movie' (their description not mine) than digging into a bowl of just popped popcorn, or chomping down on freshly fried chicken wings. To me, snow days are special times for families. C.J. would prefer a warmer less wet event for memory makers. I like Hannah, our golden, to have indoor-outdoor privileges. C.J. feels a pet's place is outside. I love flowers everywhere in our yard. C.J. objects every time he sees another flower garden developed, because it's just more work for him. For me, bills need to be paid as soon as they come in. C.J. feels closer to the payment due date is soon enough. Is this what you're talking about?"

"Absolutely," Jane responded.

I smiled as Leeta identified her list of differences between her and me, since she has had her way on all of them, except for Travis and me eating in the family room when watching certain programs and the bill payment schedule.

"You're smiling, C.J.?"

"Yes. Leeta's right about our differences, most of which have been worked out in her favor."

"Is that a problem?"

"Not really. I got my way on eating sometimes in the den and paying the bills. In fact, now Leeta eats in the den." I grinned.

"So you worked out a balance?"

Leeta nodded her head in agreement. "Yes, we worked out a balance."

Jane continued reflectively, "A lot of your marital work together has been directed toward negotiating the balance with the living issues. But, what is as important as the living issues are the issues we weren't able to work out with our parents in our childhood. In our adult relationships, we're soon confronted with our undeveloped selves. My hallucination is that we're intuitively drawn to and fall in love with the person we can work out these childhood issues with. In other words, our marriage is a growing machine for us. Do you understand?"

"Well, I guess I do," I responded slowly.

"How come?" Jane queried.

"Leeta has a strong sense of family. She's really focused on making a home for Travis and me. She's adamant about family time. Friends are always welcomed and all that other 'warm and cozy' stuff, she likes to say that makes a home a home, and not just a house where you eat and sleep only."

"Hmm." Jane nodded, placing her elbow on her chair's armrest and resting her chin on her hand's folded fingers.

"What?" I asked.

"All that stuff that you love about Leeta, but at that same time drives you up the wall."

"How did you know?" I blurted out.

"You're normal. As I've said, the differences you need to learn from each other are the most difficult or challenging in the growth process for you as an individual, and for your relationship together, to make it happily all the way to the finish line, 'til death do us part.' From what you told me, there was little sense of family you had as a child, if any. Daddy stayed at work, you hid in your room shooting blanks into a telephone book or tapping on the radio to strangers. Your sister got pregnant and left the house altogether. If I remember correctly, you described your mother as self-absorbed with a tongue like a double-edge sword. I think the only constant with your life now is you."

"Huh?"

"You're still in your room tapping on the ham radio to strangers."

* * *

"Do you want to talk about today's session?" Leeta asked me.

"Sure." *Not really,* I mused. *Yes, I know, Lord, I need to show up and be there.* "But will you give me a few minutes to finish my contact with this fella and sign off?"

"Uh huh. I'm going to make some hot tea. Want me to make you some?"

"Sounds good."

I finished listening to Jack in Kansas describe his station setup, which was actually very nice. He ran a new computer-based ham rig called the SDR 7000, where most of the actual work was done in computer software. It was the newest technology used to communicate via one of the oldest, Morse Code. No doubt, this was an interesting contact. Most of the time, radio talk was about the weather, each other's copy or how old you were. I was always impressed with the eighty-year-olds still doing strong copy. I usually got some great story about their service time during World War II. Hannah came bounding in with her usual happy self. I knew Leeta wouldn't be far behind. I quickly described my station, and that I needed to QRT, short hand for "need to end my transmission." Ending with the usual ham radio "73" and dit, ditditdit, dit.

Leeta walked in holding two mugs of hot tea and handed me one of them. She sat down in the chair beside the rig and held her warm mug between her hands. "Well." She sighed. "I had no idea, C.J., about your childhood."

"Yeah, and not something I want to rehash, Leeta."

"I get that, but I found it useful in understanding some of our issues, especially about the money and your seeming obsession with the ham radio and the Volvo."

"Yes, and talking about it with Jane helped me also. I really didn't know that what I was accusing you of were my fears, which I was projecting onto you. I'm sorry."

"Thank you, C.J. I do want you to know, I appreciate everything you've done for Travis and me. There is no doubt, C.J., our lives are enriched because of you. I've been amiss in not thanking you. I guess I assumed that you knew by the stuff I do."

"Leeta, in many ways, my mother was a good housewife like you, in that the house was well kept and good meals on the table. I do believe my father would have said the same. It was just the 'we' was left out of the equation. I remember my mother yelling at Peg, 'What do you want from me? I'm a good wife and mother. Don't you have clean clothes to wear every day, a clean home and hot meals?' And Peg yelled back, 'You, Mother, we want you! We want you to want *us* and you don't!'"

"So you need to know I want to be with you, you need to hear me say I love you and you need me to physically love you too," Leeta stated softly.

"Well . . . yes, I do."

"You need me to understand you are doing the best you can."

"Yes."

"To know when enough is enough."

"Yes."

"Done."

Chapter Twenty
I Know I Have Your Love

I ROLLED OVER IN THE BED, REACHED FOR LEETA AND GRABBED air instead. Only the bright yellow light of the bedside digital clock, outlining the time, seven-fifteen, stared back at me. I sat up in the dark and spied Hannah still asleep, curled up tightly in her corner bed. The bathroom light shone through the slight opening at the bottom of its door. I heard no motion from the bathroom, not even the sound of running water. Everything was quiet except for Hannah's soft breathing of a deep, restful sleep. I looked warily down to see our perfectly finished, but cold wood floors. Another one of our differences, which somehow was negotiated in Leeta's favor. "No, we can't cover up these beautiful hardwood floors with carpet. People pay a fortune to have wood floors in their homes, and we already have them," Leeta had said, when I said I wanted at least our bedroom floor carpeted. "What are you talking about, Leeta? When I was growing up, Mother couldn't wait until we could afford to cover all of our wood floors. I want warm, cushiony carpet to grace my feet when I get out of bed in the morning, especially when I get up to pee in the middle of night."

I winced when my feet touched the cold floor. I cradled my chilled chest with my arms for warmth, racing speedily on my tiptoes to the bathroom. "Jeez, Leeta," I fussed as I opened the door and mercifully felt a burst of warm air. The bathroom heater was on, and my clothes lay across a wooden towel rack. *Thank you, Leeta.* I sighed as I quickly put on my toasty jeans. I splashed my face with warm water, gave my teeth a quick brushing and smoothed down my hair with my hands. I smiled, looking at the man in the mirror. I no longer saw dark circles framing gray, empty eyes. The deep wrinkles still stretched across my forehead, but no complaining. I liked what I saw.

I heard a quiet knock at the bathroom door, and then it opened. There stood Leeta with her finger pressed to her lips. She mouthed, "Let's not wake the four-legged child or she would get the two-legged one up for sure." She leaned close to me, gave me a kiss and whispered, "Come with me, my knight. I have work for you for tonight's office party." Leeta held my hand as she led me quietly down the back stairs to a well-lit and inviting kitchen that smelled of fresh brewed coffee and oranges. She pointed to the cake, which sat on the far corner of the kitchen counter, "Coffee with a slice of coffee cake and a bowl of sliced oranges and grapefruit?"

"Sure."

She placed the cake in front of me and handed me the cake knife. "You cut the cake, and I'll dish out the fruit."

"Sure," I said again.

Leeta picked up the coffee pot and tilted it toward my mug. "Coffee?"

"Sure."

"C.J.?" Leeta laughed. "What's going on with you?"

"Well, I'm deciding whether I should give you a Chanukah present or an early Christmas present now."

"Chanukah?"

David said today was the first day of Chanukah, and tomorrow is Christmas Eve.

"Hmm, I'll make it easy for you. I'll take both."

"I hoped that was what you would say." I looked at her, and she never looked so beautiful. "Stay here," I said as I pushed back my chair and walked briskly to the ham radio room. Opening up the desk drawer, I retrieved an envelope and a gift-wrapped package. When I returned, Leeta had placed a piece of cake on my plate, a small bowl of fruit beside it and my mug filled with coffee next to them. She had done the same for herself and was waiting for me to join her.

"Cake first or the presents?" I asked teasingly.

"Are you kidding?" she said, holding her hand out. "Hmm, this is so good." I took a bite of the cake, then another and put the gifts on the other side of me so she couldn't reach them. "Leeta, this is delicious. It's not your usual dry cake, but moist, melt-in-your-mouth delicious! Is this a new recipe?"

Leeta's face crinkled, taking her first bite of the cake. "No it isn't. It's my grandmother's recipe, but you're right, it's really good. Just like I remembered it tasting. Finally, I might have her touch."

"What's different?"

"The recipe is the same, but I must admit, I've picked up tips from Ina and Alton.

"Ina is the *Barefoot Contessa* but who's Alton?"

"Alton Brown who does *Good Eats.*"

"Oh."

"The baking tips for cakes are room temperature for the wet ingredients—eggs, butter and milk. Really cream together your butter and sugar, and don't over beat your eggs, just incorporate them. Always begin and end your batter with flour. I guess the mixing is as important as the good ingredients. Hurray for me."

"Hurray for Food TV and following the recipe."

"What?"

"Leeta, you're no chef. You're a great cook when you follow the recipe and when you don't, ugh." I screwed up my mouth with the ugh sound.

Leeta laughed. "Enough already . . . present," she said as she extended her hand again and moved her fingers impatiently.

"Ah yes, the presents, my queen." I handed her the gift-wrapped package and the envelope.

"Which first?"

"Doesn't matter. Wait, yes it does. Present first, then the envelope."

She slowly unwrapped the present as she always did, careful not to tear the ribbon or the wrapping. I wished she would just tear the present open, but I learned from the first present I ever gave her, hurry wasn't going to happen. Once again she reiterated, "These moments cannot be rushed; every detail needs to savored and remembered. They're the memory creators to make the good times even better, and the hard times palpable. Besides, the wrapping is so beautiful. It's a shame to only use it once."

"C.J.!" She looked up with tears already filling her eyes. She held a checkbook in her hands. "Thank you, thank you," she cried as she took my hand, pulling me close to her, and gave me a soft kiss on my lips. She then opened the envelope agilely, not to tear it, and took out the folded page inside. She began reading aloud my handwritten letter:

Dear Leeta,
    Forgive me for ever letting you think I did not trust you or that I did not want you as a full partner in my life. We now have joint checking and savings accounts, and I have already contacted a lawyer about our will. We can go to the DMV office after the

New Year, sooner if you like, and get the truck put in your name.

Although the plant and its assets need to be kept separate, as it is a corporation, I will fully apprise you of the entire financial goings on. Just as my heart is now an open book to you, so are all my possessions and operations. All I ask in return is your understanding and forgiveness. I know I have your love.

88, C.J.

"Oh C.J., thank you," Leeta said quietly.

Chapter Twenty-One
New Beginnings

"Happy New Year everyone!" Kate sang out as she took off her coat and placed a white, square, cardboard box on the coffee table outside her office door. "Fresh, warm doughnuts from McFarlan, and fresh brewed coffee too in a few minutes."

My head popped out my office door, and as it did, I saw Robert and David coming from the machine area, heading directly toward the doughnuts. Robert already had a half-eaten doughnut in his hand as he reached for another. David had the newspaper safely tucked underneath his arm.

"Robert Russell, you are eating the doughnuts I brought for the fellas in the machine area," Kate scolded.

"Okay then, I'll take them one back to replace the one I took," Robert said as he flashed his signature boyish grin.

"Anybody seen today's *Times-News*?" David asked.

"Sure have," Kate said, pouring water into the coffee pot and pushing the ON button, "and the reason for our doughnut party."

David handed me the paper and pointed to the front page. The headline read, "Pristine Place." I read aloud, "Families joined the Carolina Mountain Conservancy to protect more than 3,895 acres of their land for future generations to enjoy."

"Yes sir, no golf course will ever be developed there or sprawling residential development," Kate proclaimed. "This land has been untouched, and now it will never be changed. It will keep its clear streams and old trees. It is as it was when the Cherokee lived and hunted on this very land. It will always be for the trout, deer, bear and turkey, and for our children, their children and their children after that, and to inspire their imagination and wonder." Without taking a breath, Kate reached for the white, cardboard box and asked, "Doughnut?"

"Sure." I reached for my favorite, the chocolate-covered cake doughnut. I sat down with the doughnut in my hand.

Kate pointed her finger to the left side of the front page, "And read this."

I took the paper from Kate and read the heading to the article, *Voters reject taller buildings.*

"Aloud please," Kate coaxed.

"'Sixty-four feet, tops. That's how tall seven out of ten Hendersonville voters want buildings to be downtown, based on the results of Tuesday's referendum. The outcome nullifies the vote by City Council that allowed taller buildings downtown.'"

"It's going to be a good year, yes sir!" Kate exclaimed.

I chuckled. "Yes, Kate, it's going to be a good year."

"Let's toast to that," Kate interjected. "Coffee?"

I held out my cup for her to fill, and then raised it, "New beginnings for preserving what we love and hold dear."

"Here, here," everyone said in unison.

"Finding the balance is the key variable needed to keep this promise," Robert said, touching his cup to mine with a soft ping.

"Hear, hear," everyone said in unison.

"Commitment to this balance will keep what we cherish forever," David pronounced.

"Here, here," everyone said again in unison.

"And . . ." Kate paused. "It ain't over until the fat lady sings," nodding at Robert and me as she touched each of our cups.

* * *

Leeta and I arrived at Jane's office early. I picked up the *Times-News* and the words stretched across the front page: "N.C. LAWMAKERS' VOTE LEAVES COUNCIL WITH MIXED FEELINGS."

Leeta leaned over toward me. "C.J., what does the article itself say?"

"Well, it depends on which councilman is being quoted. One of the councilmen says, 'I wish the legislators would leave the city government alone. We are elected to make decisions. I don't know why they should restrict us.'"

"Good grief," Leeta said hotly. "If our elected officials listen to the will of the people, Senator Tom would have never become involved."

"Okay, Leeta. I hear enough of this from Kate."

"Well, she's right," Leeta quickly interjected. "Read on, please."

"Another councilman states, 'I was one of the council members who wanted to see the height stay the same. Sixty-four feet is good for the downtown area. Outside of the downtown, I am open to see raising the height in the future. I don't have a problem with the legislators' decision. When we had a referendum on the issue, there was an overwhelming number of residents who wanted the height to stay the same.'"

"Well, I don't know about that. The height ordinance outside the downtown area doesn't need to be changed either," Leeta stated passionately. "We don't need to live in a high-rise bowl. Look what happened in Charlotte. Greedy developers built mammoth condo high-rises with wings jutting out into old established neighborhoods, and local government allowed it. The high-rises dwarfed the surrounding houses and created major traffic issues."

"When did you become the expert on Charlotte's infrastructure and politics?" I asked.

"My cousin and her family do live in Charlotte, remember? When Travis was a baby, we moved to Charlotte. I worked in Gastonia. It took me only thirty minutes to commute to Gastonia to work and return to Charlotte after work. When I visited my cousin this fall, I-85 was like a parking lot during the rush hours, taking two to three times longer for me to get where I wanted to go. Charlotte used to have the wonderful feel of being a small town inside of a big city. No more. I'll never go back. My cousin will have to come to Hendersonville if she wants to see me." Leeta sarcastically asked, "What did our fine mayor say?"

I smiled, looking at my beloved from over the top of the newspaper. "Let me see. He says he feels high-rises would have brought people to the downtown area by having residents downtown. He feels downtown living would have helped curb some of the growth occurring in the county."

"Oh please, how ignorant does he think the townfolk are to buy that line of reasoning? That's almost as good as the 'bigger the better' argument for the 115-foot high-rise first proposed for downtown living."

The door opened and out came Jane and a couple. No one was smiling. "Don't hesitate to call if you choose to reschedule," Jane said quietly, opening the office outside door and closing it behind the couple as they walked out. She turned toward us and smiled. "How were the holidays?"

"Do you need a break before you start with us?" I asked.

"No, thank you."

"How can you do it?"

"What do you mean?"

"Switch gears from one couple to another?"

"After thirty some years and doing the work I love to do, I just do. But I don't see more than six clients a day to make sure that happens."

I reflected, *So balance, experience and work you love to do, the cornerstone to any successful relationship, be it with your spouse, your community or your work.* "It's been a great two weeks. I can't ever remember the holidays being so joyous."

"Everything flowed," Leeta chimed in. "We celebrated everything, including Chanukah."

"You celebrated both holidays?"

Leeta laughed merrily. "We did at our holiday office party, since Chanukah began the day before Christmas Eve. David Jacobs, one of C.J.'s partners, brought the potato latkes, Chanukah gelt and dredles, his guitar and songs. My favorite song David sang was 'Light One Candle.'"

I smiled from ear to ear just watching Leeta. I remembered another reason why I fell in love with her. Her joy was infectious.

"One of my favorite songs too," Jane said softly, motioning us into the counseling room. We sat down in our respective chairs. "The second verse to the song is very fitting for the two of you."

"How does that verse go?" I asked, curious to what the words were. I liked the song too. All I could remember was the chorus, which was catchy.

Jane began effortlessly saying the words:

> Light one candle for the strength that we need
>> To never become our own foe
> And light one candle for those who are suffering
>> Pain we learned so long ago
> Light one candle for all we believe in
>> That anger not tear us apart
> And light one candle to find us together
>> With peace as the song in our hearts."

Leeta looked at me through her chocolate brown eyes. "That is a good song for us, along with the chorus, especially the last two lines, 'Don't let the light go out. Let it shine through our love and our tears.'"

Jane nodded her head and smiled. "In last session, we talked about your family and the session before that, we discussed money management. Where to begin?"

"Well, I think Leeta and I've *negotiated* . . ." I meticulously emphasized negotiated, "a good solution for our money issue and as far as my family and my mother, it is what it is, and I'm okay with it."

"So what did you negotiate?"

"An open book to my personal and business accounts; we now have a joint checking and savings account. I've made a date with a lawyer for our Will and for a title transfer for the truck after the New Year."

"And you?" Jane asked Leeta.

"The same, but my stuff is nowhere as involved as his—a monthly child support check and what I've earned from training horses. But yes, everything is an open book. I want C.J. to know my income and my expenses. I've wanted to do this for a long time."

"Transparency with your monies is an excellent first step, but there is one more step in resolving your money management concerns with each other."

"Transparency, good word." Leeta chuckled. "All books are now open."

"Yes, and now you two need to decide on a process, a plan on how you want to spend and save your money."

"Any suggestions?" I asked.

"Not really," Jane popped back, "there's no right or wrong way, but you both must feel balanced with whatever process you decide on. Transparency and an agreed-upon process are the keys to money management challenges between partners. This needs to be thoughtfully *negotiated.*" Jane grinned, as she too meticulously emphasized negotiated. "Money matters between couples are the number one reason for divorce, if they are not worked out."

"So we have a lot more work to do," Leeta said.

"Sure do, and that's a homework assignment for next session. You have the tools now to negotiate this out on your own."

Yeah . . . great tools . . . we just have to commit to using them, I thought.

Jane turned and faced me directly. The smile had left her face, and her tone had softened. "C.J., do you mind sharing what has changed that you're now okay with your family and mother?"

"Well, I guess because that's in the past. I'm no longer in that family situation and never will be again, and Leeta is not my mother. I did know and I did not know that I was attracted to Leeta for her strong values about family. Am I making any sense, Jane, at all with what I just said?"

"Yes, you make a great deal of sense."

"She demonstrates daily her love of family and me in everything she does. You're right, I do have a lot to learn from her. Oh yes, you're right again. Exactly what I fell in love with, this family-together thing and all, drives me up the *wall*." The words, BAD APPROACH, suddenly flashed in big bold red neon lights in my mind's eye, and the words "but not all the time," shot out of my mouth. The avalanche of words tumbled out of my mouth, as in the last session. There was no way to stop them now. I just hoped they wouldn't bury me. I grinned sheepishly, as I cut my eyes over to Leeta.

Jane chuckled. Leeta placed her hands over her mouth to hide her smile; then she threw back her head and cackled with laughter until tears ran down her cheeks.

"What?" I feigned surprise, as my chest released on its own a breath of relief. *I didn't piss her off. Her laughter is back too, her unrestrained great laugh.*

"Great," Jane broke in. "Laughter is good. It tells me that the healing has begun between the two of you, and that you two now have some degree of flexibility with each other, a needed ingredient in working out your living issues. But C.J., you need to do one other thing to let go of the past, so it doesn't interfere with yours and Leeta's relationship ever again."

"What's that?"

"You need to forgive your mother."

"Forgive her for being a . . . w-w-witch?" I stopped short, straining not to say the "B" word. She is or was my mother, after all. I didn't know if she still was alive. "It's been seventeen years since my holiday card was returned to me unopened and stamped 'return to sender, no such addressee.'" I stopped short as my brain projected a mental picture of a much younger man holding an envelope in his hand, reading and rereading the words stamped across his mother's name and address. *What did I do or not do that prompted my mother to eliminate me from her life?*

"Yes, forgive her," Jane stated in her usual persistent but calm manner. "Let me say it this way: I firmly believe what human beings do is the best they can do—"

"You're kidding," I interrupted. "That was the best she could do? Why in the hell did she have two children? She should've quit with Peg."

"Let me finish please, and you need to breathe, C.J., so you can stay in front brain," Jane insisted.

"Okay." I took a deep slow breath in and released it, feeling the stress leave my body.

"Thank you. As I was saying, I believe people do the best they can do with the information they have at the time and the options they think are available to them. I don't know what your mother's life experiences were before she met your dad. But they had to be troublesome, or she would not have made the choices she made in her marriage with your father, and with you and Peg."

"What do you mean?"

"I question whether her childhood was nurturing, because of her difficulty in loving her children and her husband, her being dismissive and at the same time competitive in her relationship with Peg and with your father. I could be wrong, for I don't have all the information about your mother, but it doesn't matter, she's not here. You are."

I nodded my head in agreement. The little I knew about my mother's childhood was difficult. Her grandmother raised her because her mother spent most of her life in and out of a psychiatric hospital. Her father was married at least four times that I know of and killed himself by placing a pistol in his mouth. "You're correct, her childhood wasn't easy. My grandfather killed himself. I was little, still in elementary school. It was summer, and we had just returned home from a two-week family vacation at the beach. I was in bed when the phone rang and then, I remember my mother's screams. I was too afraid to get out of the bed."

"Uh huh," Jane said quietly.

"So I need to call her, or visit her?"

"No, I didn't say that at all. That's up to you. Forgiveness doesn't mean you'll ever excuse what she did, but once you decide to forgive her, you'll feel—

"Sorry for her, not angry," I interrupted completing Jane's sentence.

"Yes or compassion, and by doing this, you can begin to heal your childhood wounds, another ingredient needed to separate your relationship with Leeta from your mother."

"Hmm, all of this is coming at me fast, but I think I understand what you're saying."

"I don't expect you to get this all at once, but you will in time. I do feel you have a good beginning to fix the cracks in your pillar. We have one more issue to put on the table, which we've only dabbled with in the beginning of our work together."

"Oh yes," Leeta blurted out, "the every-seven-second-phenomenon sex." She had a grin that spread across her beautiful face. "Well, I think we've made headway in that department. You agree, C.J.?"

"Much improved, but . . ." I hesitated, fearful that what I really wanted to say could stop the progress, which had already been made with our sex life.

"Gracious, don't tell me you want even more?" Leeta gasped.

Might as well "tell the truth, nothing but the truth," and Jane Levy's office is the safest place to do it, I thought. *Besides, working out my stuff with Leeta is only going to be as good as the information I give her.* "Yes," I said awkwardly.

"You're kidding. The seven-second phenomenon is for real." Leeta had now turned toward me and faced me directly. However, she had calmed down considerably from her initial gasp. Jane sat motionless. I knew we were on our own to negotiate this living issue. It was time. I was ready.

"What is your fantasy then?" Leeta queried.

"Every day of the week would be just fine."

"Every day of the week," Leeta said slowly, as she was trying to absorb the full essence of what I was saying.

Well, the box was opened. I might as well continue. Just hope I was opening the lost treasure chest and not Pandora's Box. "Yes, my fantasy is four days of the week I would like to have sex for the sport of it plus one day your way, one day my way, and one day we make love." I grinned cautiously.

Jane gave a hearty laugh. Leeta sat quietly and mouthed to herself, "Four times a week for the sport of it."

"Are you surprised?" I asked Leeta.

"No, I guess not."

"Well?"

"I don't know. I don't know if I'll have the stamina for every day of the week."

"You appeared to have the stamina when we were dating. What changed?"

"One thing, we didn't date every night of the week."

"Close to it."

"It was different."

"What was different?" *Take it easy C.J.,* I thought, as one more question shot out of my mouth. We both stopped and stared at each other. My quiet thought was, *Our lives were just as busy back then, as they are now.*

"I don't know." Leeta whispered. Again, we stared at each other, waiting for the other to say something.

"Just a theory here," Jane gently interjected. "When you were dating, you were at the top of each other's list."

"Instead of dropped off the list," I stated.

"I don't understand, C.J.," Leeta retorted. "That has been my issue with *you,* being on the bottom of your priority list."

"Yes, I know, but my priority list is different from yours. I miss our intimate time together. Yes, it has much improved, but nowhere near like it was when we dated. We dated for two years, Leeta. Granted, we didn't go out all the time. But we always had our 'porch time' together, after Travis's homework was done, his bath, his bedtime story read and him to bed. Remember, that was what you called our time together in the evening. Now we have a porch, which wraps around most of the house. I have no memory of us sitting on it together, ever. Our sex life was rich and full. What happened to it when we got married?"

"I-I." Leeta stopped. She cast her eyes downward. "We got busy with life, renovating the house, Travis, building a new business."

"But, Leeta, that's *your* life not *ours*. What happened to ours?" I responded in kind.

Leeta sat in her chair motionless. The quiet slowly filled up the room like molasses being poured into a jar.

"I guess I'm afraid. In my first marriage . . . after we got married . . . my husband disappeared to go hunting or out with his guy friends. The only time he wanted to be with me was for sex. In this marriage, soon after we got married, you immersed yourself in your work and hobbies of the ham radio and constant repair work with your Volvo. I reached out to you more than once to have some porch time, and you would say, 'Let me just finish this . . . I'll be there in a minute.' And many an evening I sat on the porch by myself . . . and then I just stopped asking . . ."

Her voice became a whisper and dropped off. *Oh, my gosh. I remember her coming to the den as I was playing on the ham radio.* I looked over at Leeta. Tears were slowly falling down her cheeks.

"Well," Jane said, finally interrupting the impenetrable silence, which had now engulfed the room. "So your fear is that the only way you can be put on the top of the list is when you agree to have sex."

"Yes, I guess that's right," Leeta said, "because both my first husband and C.J. initiated the time to be with me when we were dating . . . simply wonderful times. And then it stopped. Once married, I felt invisible."

"But, Leeta," I said, "I remember asking you, 'let's take a hike and have a picnic while Travis is at school' or 'let's go up town and have lunch.' And your comment back to me was, 'I'm waiting for the contractor about the renovations for the house,' or 'I'm training a new horse. Not this time, maybe later.' So I gave up as you did, and, as you say, I *did* immerse myself at work."

"I guess I did put you off too. Now I realize I was afraid that this would be a repeat of my first marriage . . . being alone . . . married and lonely."

"Frequently in relationships," Jane said, "couples come in with their unresolved issues of the past. Unwittingly, either or both will trigger that heartache of each other's past . . . and then it becomes a couple's issue when it never should have been. Like you, C.J. Your unresolved issues of your mother were being dumped on Leeta."

Leeta, with soft, caring eyes, stated, "I realize now I sabotaged our wonderful times together . . . like the evening after the Christmas ride . . . when I shut you down and walked away. Completely abandoning hot chocolate and cookies on the couch in front of the fire."

"So you each bring issues to the table," Jane responded. "You each need to work on your part of the dance."

Leeta turned to me with her eyes sparkling. "So now, we're ready to talk about sex."

I smiled with relief. "I am so ready."

Jane laughed. "Ready, set, GO! A book I read some time ago, authored by a woman, stated men's idea of foreplay misses the mark. C.J., any idea what is required to woo Leeta into your bed?"

"Take it slow, and it all comes fast. I read that somewhere, or did you tell me that, Leeta?" I grinned at Leeta, remembering one of our recent evenings together.

Jane guffawed, "Well, yes, that sounds like a winner. But generally for women, it's foreplay from the time they get up in the morning to the time they go to bed at night."

"What do you mean?" I asked.

"C.J., you're already doing it by making yourself emotionally available and being helpful when you're home. You did say your sex life is much improved?"

"Yes, but sometimes I don't want to follow the script. I do want sex for the sport of it. I don't want to do the dance all day long for the cherished moment at night beneath the bed sheets. That's what made our dating so much fun. We had sex any place any time." I wondered if Leeta remembered our hikes together, when we would find ourselves in the forest alone or at some beautiful isolated mountain stream or waterfall. Often she would take off her clothes, as if she wanted nothing to interfere between the natural lushness that surrounded us and me. She was so comfortable in her own skin. I never dreamed I would want anyone as much as I wanted Leeta.

"Leeta, apparently you do know what C.J. is talking about. Right?"

"Yes, I do."

Jane continued, "And for men, sex is the best way for them to connect emotionally with whom they love. Without sex, men can feel just as alone and lonely as you just described feeling."

"Yes." Leeta's jaw had tightened now. "C.J., sex every night of the week, I'm overwhelmed, even with the thought of it. Last week alone, we had sex at least four times minimum. Gosh, one day, I think we had sex twice, one time 'for the sport of it,' as you say, while Travis took his shower."

"Okay, you're right. I love steak too, but not every night. Sex every night would be too much for me also." I grinned. "I might die from exhaustion."

"Maybe what I really want from you is for you to be more proactive," I said. "If the truth be known, what I miss most from our dating is your pursuing me, your sexual creative spontaneity, not the frequency. You know, you seduced me sometimes—not me always being the initiator. Remember?"

"I remember," Leeta acknowledged quietly.

"Okay, you two, this is a good beginning, and this dialogue needs to continue at home together," Jane announced.

"Another homework assignment?" I asked.

"Exactly. As I've already said, you have tools now to keep the communication doors wide open and the talk flowing. But, I need to give you more information for this assignment. Leeta, when C.J. helps you around the house, how do you feel?"

"Appreciated, and . . . that he really loves me and cares about me. Like for the holiday party at the house, he helped me all day long getting ready, and with the clean-up afterward. Just thinking about it almost makes me cry."

"You felt loved and appreciated?"

"Exactly."

"And sex, for men, along with their wives *initiating* the sex, makes them feel exactly the same way, loved and appreciated. Men are not as emotionally expressive as women regarding love and appreciation. They show their love and appreciation with their bodies. Without that connection, they can feel as lonely as the wives do when they are not talked to or listened to."

"Right on," I blurted out.

"Leeta, from what C.J. says, you've been quite the seductress. All you need to do is retrieve it."

Leeta looked over at me. Her eyes were soft and loving. "So sex for men is what long stem roses and candlelight dinners are for women."

Jane smiled. "Well, yes, that's a good way to say it."

"Hmm," Leeta said. "We'll find our balance again, and we're on our own to work it out. We've graduated," she stated, looking out of her chocolatey brown eyes, right into mine.

"Yes, you've graduated. Congratulations. Sessions now will center on the work you do at home. Assessing what works and what needs improvement," Jane said, as she stood up and directed us to the waiting room door. As she opened it, there sat Robert in the same chair with the same familiar look I had that October day not too long ago. Robert and I both nodded at one another, and as I carefully closed the outside door behind us, I heard Jane say, "Hello, may I help you?"

Leeta said, "Yes, she can," as she took my hand.

I turned her around and pulled her close to me. As I did, I felt a soft, feather-like touch brush across my cheek. "Yes, we can and all the way to the finish line, 'till death do us part,'" I whispered into Leeta's ear.

Epilogue

My dearest Leeta,

My love for you is timeless.
It grows day by day, second by second.
Soon it shall fill all the universe,
And be just as limitless.
88, C.J.